In Shady Groves

"Your men consort with temple prostitutes, and your rulers love shameful ways. You have sown the wind—and you will reap the whirlwind!"

Spoken with the quick-burning voice of God, here is Hosea's prophetic message to the people of Israel—a nation caught in a web of degradation and greed.

But Hosea himself, scorned as a hypocrite, is suffering tremendous inner anguish—for all Israel knows he is bound by an endless, aching love for a pagan priestess!

In these pages you will see the unfolding of God's divine plan as Hosea, belittled and hated by his countrymen, is called to be a living example of God's forgiving love for an adulterous land.

In Shady Groves

Yvonne Lehman

Published by
chosen books
FLEMING H. REVELL COMPANY
OLD TAPPAN, NEW JERSEY

Library of Congress Cataloging in Publication Data

Lehman, Yvonne.
In shady groves.
1. Hosea, the Prophet—Fiction. I. Title.
PS3562.E4316 1983 813'.54 83-7431
ISBN 0-310-60670-5

ISBN 0-8007-9143-6

A Chosen Book

Chosen Books are published by
Fleming H. Revell Company
Old Tappan, New Jersey
Printed in the United States of America

Prologue

The Lord was angry with Israel. He had guided His chosen people out of Egypt to the Promised Land. But His people had not been grateful. Or obedient.

Through the prophets—Isaiah, Jeremiah, Ezekiel, Hosea—God had thundered His warnings. But the people of Israel continued to seek pleasure and lead sinful lives.

Then God said to Hosea: "Go and marry; your wife will be unfaithful. . . . This will show how my people have left me and become unfaithful" (see Hosea 1:2).

As always, God had a momentous plan for His people.

In Shady Groves

Chapter One

Walking to the edge of the cliff, Hosea spotted in the valley below the distant figure racing toward him. As always, he was entranced by her lithe young body and agility of foot. Then he took a deep breath and set his face straight ahead. The weight of what he had to tell Gomer lay upon his shoulders like the leaden sky pressing down upon the distant hills.

He had a right—yes, a duty—to see that this beautiful child not become another victim of an outrageous pagan custom by which temple priests culled the choicest young females. They selected girls without blemish, like lambs for slaughter. Gomer herself was truly a jewel. Her young body held the promise of a lovely flower in bloom.

Hosea lifted his hand in response to Gomer, who waved at him. Smiling now, he recalled the first time he had seen her months before. He had wandered far from home on his donkey to this exact spot, where he had been mesmerized by the melodic tones emanating from a group of children gathered around the well below. Their young teacher, playing a golden lyre, had looked up suddenly at him, and without hesitation waved. He waved back and went down to meet her. She and the children, he discovered, were from nearby Bethel, a fast-growing town with numerous pagan temples and fashionable, pleasure-seeking people.

Gomer had induced Hosea to join their circle. He held her soft, slender hand when they danced in a circle with the children. Her hand remained in his a brief second longer than necessary after the game. It occurred to him that Marabah would have lowered her eyes and blushed. Gomer stared at him unflinching, with an expression brazenly akin to adoration. He'd never seen eyes that color, nor so expressive. Quickly he reminded himself that she was little more than a child. They began meeting each week at this same place, sometimes without the children.

Now he did not reach out for her hand as she ascended to the brow of the hill. Dancing eyes met his and breathless laughter escaped through parted lips. Even the graying light could not shade her beauty.

"What do you find so amusing, little dove?"

Obviously delighted by his term of endearment, Gomer turned her head, allowing the fingers of wind to brush her long black hair away from her glowing face, warm from the long walk. "We always come to watch the sun set, Hosea," she teased. "It hasn't shone for weeks."

Hosea laughed. Her playful tone momentarily expelled the gloom that had settled within his breast. "To watch you is to see the sun rise," he countered lightly.

Gomer's gleaming eyes narrowed slightly. "You have honey in your mouth tonight, sir. I must have been right. Down by the well I looked up and saw the wind tugging at your garment. You looked so tall, so handsome, so majestic, I wondered were you not a god, commanding this impending storm to cease and the sun to burst forth."

Laughing, Hosea shook his head, turned and found a dry, rocky spot to sit upon. Their lighthearted bantering was like a ritual, he thought. It kept them from facing uncomfortable reality. He was a Hebrew. Devout Hebrews did not speak to women in public. So she played the child, which somehow had made their meetings acceptable. Until now, at least.

Shivering in the windy gale, Gomer slid gracefully into her customary place beside him, her knees bent and shapely bare legs drawn up against her thighs. Her slender body, braced by one hand on the flattened hilltop, leaned toward him. But she remained silent. Sometimes Hosea would tell her what bothered him. When he could not meet her, he usually explained that he had been meeting the demands of his priestly duties, delivering freshly baked bread for his mother or working in the fields with his father.

The wind picked up and clouds hastened toward the valley. They must not linger, but Hosea knew she would stay until he bade her go. A sad smile touched his lips. "We may not see each other for a while, little dove."

His sideways glance barely caught her eye. He saw her rub at the spatters of mud on her legs and noticed her dirt-caked feet. It had been three weeks since they had last met. Her voice was thin. "Why?"

"You know I'm studying to become a priest."

She nodded, then looked down beside him and picked up a pebble from a patch of weeds struggling for a home on the rocky ledge. The moisture in the air hung heavily. He cleared his throat. "My vows will be taken. There will be much activity. It is expected that my marriage to Marabah will soon follow."

With a quick movement, Gomer flung the pebble through space until she heard it land on the rocky surface below. Then she jumped to her feet, striking a careless pose, her hands on her hips.

"Marabah!" she exclaimed. "Is she pretty? Does she sing? Does she laugh a lot? Will she give you babies?" She sucked in her breath. "Do you like her better than me?"

Dear God, he moaned inwardly. Could she be playing a game to make him laugh? No, he could not deny the misery in her eyes and the pain in her voice. How could he answer the questions that had tumbled out? Marabah had been part of his life for almost two dozen years. He had become betrothed to her while still in his mother's womb. Marabah was . . . Marabah! She was good, dedicated to their God Jehovah, an excellent cook, an intelligent woman, and would be a devoted mate for a man.

Gomer, on the other hand, was a raven-haired girl with flashing violet eyes, clear, smooth skin and pink-flushed cheeks, who danced and sang with children. Her lilting laughter remained long after she was gone. Only children laughed as she did. She was a bright spot in a troubled world. But Gomer lived in Bethel.

Did he like Marabah better? He could not entertain such a question. To answer would change nothing. Looking up, he observed a frightened little girl who trembled as the wind played havoc with her long black hair and the hem of her short tunic. A sudden tenderness struck his heart. "How old are you, child?"

Stricken, her eyes turned toward the sea of clouds, riding on waves of wind that carried her voice to Hosea's ears. "I'm seventeen. Closer to eighteen. I could have been married years ago." In the gray world about them, only her eyes blazed with color. He could not look away from them when she walked closer. Her voice was steady now. "I'm not a child, Hosea. I'm a woman."

He struggled with this idea. When did a young girl become a woman? When she began her monthly cleansing? Or when. . . . He did not complete the thought.

She did it for him. "I am married to the gods."

To still the trembling in his body, Hosea pulled his knees

close and hugged the robe over them, as if to brace himself from an onslaught. What exactly did that mean? There were rumors, of course, but he could not think those things of her.

Taking her place beside him again, she asked softly, "Do you know what I'm saying?"

"No!"

Gomer gasped at the violence of his shout as it echoed around the hills and was joined by the rumbling of thunder. His world was spinning and her words were ringing in his ears. With elbows on his knees, he pressed his hands to his temples and closed his eyes to stop the swirling world.

Her desperate words reached him. "It's not some terrible thing, Hosea. Being a woman is an honor, something wonderful. Can you not understand? Are you not a man?"

Not a man? he thought. If respect for one's betrothed was not a man, then no. If preferring to spill one's seed in the privacy of his own need, rather than taking a whore, was not manly, then no, he was not a man. If honor and control and obedience to God's demands meant nothing, then no, he was not a man. He wondered why she had met him here, every week, weather permitting, for almost a year. And why had he?

"Have my words meant nothing to you?" he pleaded, misery in his voice.

"Which words, Hosea?"

Which words? he was thinking. All the stories he had told her about how God led the Hebrews out of Egypt and made a great nation of them. Gomer had listened intently but often laughed at points he had not intended to be humorous. He was not sure she had believed the stories about the parting of the waters of the Red Sea, nor the leading of the cloud by day and the pillar of fire by night. He had prayed his words would have an impact. Had she sensed some silent communication his lips had not uttered, this woman-child?

Struggling against the emotions surging within, he wrenched the words from his throat. "About God Jehovah. All the stories I told you. His promises, His commandments!"

"Yes," she assured him in a trembly voice, obviously unable to fathom his distress. "I like Him. I even thought"—she said the words haltingly—"that after you are a priest, we might worship together."

He jumped to his feet. "I am not that kind of priest! I serve the one true God." His voice echoed with the rumbling heavens.

In an instant Gomer was on her feet, too. Indignation shook her body and defiance darkened her violet eyes. "I will pretend no more to try to please you. I say there are many gods and yours is a minor one."

Dismayed shock consumed him. "You dare to blaspheme God?"

"Blaspheme? I said I liked Him. But my gods are as real as yours." Then out of her mouth poured the details of things he did not want to hear. She stopped only when his body and face became as silent stone.

Hosea was now totally convinced of Gomer's dedication, as his eyes raked her face and trembling body. He no longer saw the child and could not abide the woman.

"Please," she implored meekly, the fight gone from her.

Stepping back, Hosea shunned the outstretched hand as if it were leprous. For several moments he stood there clenching and unclenching his fists, his forehead furrowed, his golden brown eyes now dark. What could he say? Don't return to Bethel? It was too late for that. Where could she go? To Ephraim? No, for his people stoned women like Gomer.

And why should she leave Bethel, anyway? Had she not just convinced him of her fervor for the so-called gods? She was no longer a virgin, had apparently seen a newborn baby sacrificed, and considered herself highly honored. Things done to young girls, innocent babies and the population in general under the guise of god-worship were abominable. A deafening rumble in the hills made him suddenly, gratefully, aware of the threatening elements. Rain began striking their skin and clothing.

"Hurry home now. There's a storm upon us." His voice was labored, his face as gray as the clouds. His forceful "Hurry!" seemed to hurl her down the hillside, as carelessly as if he had thrown a pebble.

Gomer slid, slipped, stumbled once, but kept her balance. Upon reaching the well, she broke into a run, her bare feet making prints in the mud being spattered with the sudden deluge. The wind whipped the light linen tunic about her thighs. Black hair swirled about her head and shoulders. The beautiful dove he had found at the well was a woman, with her face set toward Bethel.

Chapter Two

As Hosea watched Gomer scamper down the hillside, a feeling of black despair closed over him. With clenched fists, he lifted his face toward the heavens, now boiling with menacing dark clouds. Angrily he reached to the neck of his robe and ripped it to the waist. The wind caught the long garment as if to strip it from his body. Rain beat upon his bare chest.

Nearby his donkey brayed and Hosea began to comprehend the gloomy, swirling world about him. He was grateful that the donkey would lead him home, even in the driving rain.

Always before, Baalism had been but a concept to him. Now it was reality. Had he not heard they took girls at a very early age? Could he be so foolish as to believe they would spare such a beautiful one? Or was it his own mind that refused to see her differently?

"How else could I justify the time spent with her? Or the thoughts I could not keep from my mind?" he asked himself aloud as he climbed onto his donkey and urged the beast on through the mire and over slippery rocks. "I am to be a priest. And will soon be a married man. My only justification would be to convince her of the reality of the one true God. In that, I failed."

The donkey sensed his way through the hills now obscured

by the downpour and early darkness. An hour later it stopped at the stones surrounding the property of Hosea's father, Beeri, who had acquired land and built a home outside Jerusalem. Slipping off the donkey, Hosea sank into mud that covered his leather sandals. He took them off and, holding onto the donkey, made his way to the shelter behind the main house. After rubbing the donkey down and giving him food in a warm corner, Hosea walked outside again into the wind, rain and rolling thunder, while jagged white streaks lighted up the sky.

He swung open the great wooden gate of the stone wall and entered the courtyard. Before entering the house, he stood over a drain to clean the mud from his feet and sandals.

Deciding not to work in the fields because of the threatening weather, Beeri had helped his wife, Huldah, all afternoon in the bakery. The warmth of the loaves and cakes, as he wrapped them in soft cloths, seemed to ease the constant gnawing pain that afflicted his swollen joints.

Huldah, a slightly stooped woman with a thickening figure, checked each of the great brick ovens, making sure the doors were tightly closed. They would cool during the night, only to be fired again in the early morning for another day's baking. Huldah removed the kerchief from her head and wiped perspiration from her brow. Taking off her apron, she picked up a lamp to make her way to the kitchen to join Beeri. Just as she entered the passageway, Hosea appeared from the outside.

"Hosea, we were so worried," Huldah gushed impulsively. Cautiously reaching toward his drenched sleeve, she asked, "Where have you been? Oh, Hosea, your robe is torn!"

"Just warm some milk for him, Huldah," Beeri cautioned, coming into the passageway after lighting the kitchen lamps. One glance at his son told him Hosea was in no mood for his mother's coddling.

Obediently, Huldah went into the kitchen. Beeri's glance had reflected what he had often told her: "Hosea's a man now, Huldah." He knew what she was thinking—that it was hard to let her only son go his own way. How simple it had been years ago, when she could set him on her lap, smooth out his little furrowed brow with gentle words, a tender touch, an explanation of events, an answering to his questions.

After Hosea had peeled off his torn, wet clothing and donned a dry robe, the two went into the kitchen and pulled up stools before the fire that Beeri had lighted on the hearth. Stroking his short-cropped graying beard, Beeri glanced at Hosea from beneath bushy gray brows, uncertain how to deal with this strange mood of his son.

There had been a time, long ago, when he had expected his son to grow up and one day take over the farm. That dream had ended when Hosea, as a small child, had exhibited an unusually analytical, inquiring mind. He was proud of his son, whose education and abilities in many ways exceeded his own; but there was a part of Hosea that he did not know how to reach. Simple answers did not satisfy the young man, who seemed to find life complex.

Hosea stared at the cup in his hands. "Father," he said, "I cannot be a priest."

"Cannot be a priest?" Beeri thundered. That he would never have suspected. Priesthood had been Hosea's dream since he was a small child. Searching for an explanation, Beeri stammered, "You feel—unworthy, Hosea?"

"Who is worthy, Father?" Hosea replied immediately. "That is why we sacrifice and pray. No, I don't expect to be worthy."

The fire blazed brightly, causing dancing shadows to play across Hosea's face, revealing the tautness of his facial muscles and fine lines of strain beneath his eyes.

"It is an awesome responsibility," Beeri agreed.

Yet Beeri knew his son did not fear responsibility. Hosea

never hesitated to speak out to the people about the writings of Moses or the laws and commandments God had given. He had no reservations concerning entering the Holy of Holies, making sacrifices or praying.

Hosea spoke after a long pause, as if speaking to himself. "Our priests no longer have a word from God." The thunder outside rumbled and the lantern beside them trembled. "I feel as secure as. . . ." He gestured, indicating the shaking lantern. "As that."

Beeri put his hand on Hosea's knee. "What have you done, son?"

Hosea looked down at his bare feet. His voice was low. "That is my sin, Father. I have done nothing. I have not dashed one golden calf into little pieces. I have kept the word of God within the confines of the Temple. What good is it there?" His voice shook with emotional intensity. "What good is it to be a priest of God if it changes nothing?"

Beeri felt he was beginning to understand Hosea's feeling of inadequacy. "There are many evils in our land, Hosea," he began, clasping his fingers together and gazing into the fire. "But our priests are God's spokesmen, the stabilizing force. Without them, God would have no voice. You have always believed that you are part of that voice, Hosea."

Only the crackling of the fire was heard for a long time. Hosea's answer was barely audible. "I will think about what you've said, Father."

"If you do not become a priest, what will you do?" Beeri asked.

Hosea shrugged dejectedly and shook his head, then lifted the cup to his lips. His eyes took on a faraway, distant expression. Beeri stood and placed his large hands on Hosea's shoulders. "Son," he said, "I can't always give you answers, but I'm always willing to listen."

Hosea reached up, covered his father's hand with his own and nodded.

"Perhaps it's just one of those bad days, Hosea. Perhaps you will feel differently in the morning," Beeri added.

"I hope you're right, Father," Hosea replied.

"It is, as you say, Beeri, just an off-day for him, don't you think?" Huldah asked later when Beeri told her of his conversation with Hosea.

"I don't know, Huldah," he replied, looking at her with warm affection. "Always before, he has been so certain about his life."

Hulda sighed. She had waited many years for a child, difficult years of telling herself constantly that she might never have one. She had tried to accept it as God's will and had thrown herself into her baking, making a career of it. When Hosea was born, with both parents in their late thirties, it was like a miraculous blessing from God. Some of the happiest days of her life had been while holding that precious child in her arms. Now she longed for that again as a grandmother.

She finished brushing out the long black hair that she usually wore coiled at the nape of her neck. She was proud that there were only a few strands of gray. She had grown rather plump over the years, but Beeri assured her that was just the way he liked her. Sliding into bed beside him, she leaned over and blew out the lamp light on the bedside table, then settled against his waiting arm.

"He should have married Marabah a long time ago, Beeri," Huldah sighed wistfully. "A man his age needs a wife. I never understood why he kept postponing the marriage with silly excuses."

"Marabah would make a perfect wife," Beeri assured her, then added solemnly, "for a priest."

Chapter Three

Despite the raging storm and her motherly concern for Gomer, who was out in it somewhere, Athalia entered the dining room with her usual grace and vitality as servants put the finishing touches to the table. Her nod indicated that the family could be summoned and dinner served. Athalia's long white gown blended subtly with the decor of the room and her royal blue sash matched her husband's dark robe that she had laid out for him. She sighed. Diblaim would probably be late, too.

Athalia's deep blue eyes surveyed the room, reflecting the warm, cozy glow emitted by the wall lamps. She had never regretted turning over the mansion to her daughter Rizpah and her husband, Jothan, when they married. This house was smaller, but made a lovely home. She especially loved the dining room with its blue draperies, and the white couches with golden trim that so complemented the marble table in the center of the room. This night was a special occasion—a time to honor Rizpah, her 27-year-old daughter, who would replace her as High Priestess in the temple.

Both sadness and relief touched Athalia's heart as she thought of this change. Aging was a fact of life one must attempt to face with grace. She smiled at that. Diblaim said she was the same striking beauty as when he first saw her twenty-eight years ago. But she was now in her mid-forties and without the youthful energy of years before. The honor of having been High Priestess would always be hers, and she looked forward to retirement. She and Diblaim had plans.

Diblaim, with Rizpah beside him, entered through an archway carrying a tray of golden objects. He returned Athalia's smile. She saw with satisfaction that he had put on the dark robe. And Rizpah had had the forethought to wear a rose-colored dress that added needed color to her pale skin.

Athalia walked over to Diblaim and placed her hand on his arm. He had grown more handsome with the years as his hair turned white. He was also a businessman to be admired—the finest goldsmith in the country. His exports reached even Egypt.

Rizpah was still wan and listless, Athalia noted. It was now a month since the birth of her baby, which she had dutifully sacrificed to the gods. Having waited so long for her first child, giving him up had been especially hard. "An easy sacrifice would mean nothing to the gods," her mother had told her.

Now, as Diblaim presented her with the tray, Rizpah's face had brightened and her slightly overweight body relaxed. She listened carefully to her father's explanation. The little golden pots held oil and wicks. Their tiny lids were designed to snuff out the flames. The gold was the finest, the craftsmanship the best. But of course! It had been crafted by her father. Gratefully Rizpah kissed his cheek. He smiled, then looked at Athalia, for it was her approval he always sought.

Rizpah's blue eyes brightened again as her husband entered the room. Jothan nearly always wore black, a constant reminder that he was High Priest at Bethel Temple. That set him apart, as did his tallness. His oval face was accentuated by dark, close-cropped hair and a fine, pointed beard and mustache. His black eyes indicated intelligence and confidence.

"Jothan," Rizpah entreated, "come and see what Papa has made for us."

Jothan admired the gift as one arm slipped around Rizpah's waist. "You've outdone yourself again, Diblaim. Masterpieces!" His deep-throated compliment pleased Diblaim and Athalia, who walked to the table while servants entered with platters of food.

Athalia now expressed her concern. "I hope Gomer isn't caught somewhere in the storm."

Moving his hand from around Rizpah's waist, Jothan turned to her and shook his head. "Gomer just came in. Wet to the skin. She doesn't feel like joining us."

While instructing a servant to take food to her daughter, Athalia noted that Rizpah's face had clouded at the mention of Gomer's name. *What was happening between these two sisters?* she wondered. Gomer's breathtaking beauty was now obvious to everyone, but it should not be a threat to Rizpah. Her younger sister could hardly replace her as High Priestess. Unless, of course, Rizpah became pregnant every year. Athalia turned her attention to the dinner.

Platters of delectable food now graced the table. Servants uncovered platters. Jothan broke a piece of steaming bread, allowing the aroma to fill his nostrils. "Wonderful!" His exclamation brought a flush of pleasure to the servants.

Rizpah laughingly passed the fresh butter to him. "It's even better with this."

Athalia had a sudden thought and turned to Jothan. "Now that Gomer is an assistant at the temple, do you think she is interested in Beniah?"

Jothan shook his head. "Her interest is in a man who lives

on a farm outside of Ephraim. She speaks with him often when she takes the children to the well. And other times, too."

Athalia was as surprised as the others. "I know nothing of this. Who is this man?"

"Naturally, I have inquired." Jothan made his voice as unconcerned as possible. "He has the reputation of being a responsible, intelligent young man. He is Hosea, son of Beeri, who owns all the farmland beyond the brown hills, all the way to Ephraim."

Diblaim listened with interest. His face lit up. "I know of Beeri. His farm provides the food for Bethel and Ephraim. His crops are sold even in Jerusalem. A wealthy and prominent family. Well-respected, I understand."

Athalia leaned forward, alive with anticipation. She expected much of her family and they had never disappointed her. "I certainly want to hear more of this," she exclaimed.

A sly grin touched the corners of Jothan's mouth. "Hosea is training to become a priest."

He had the complete attention of his listeners. Where? When? Was it one of those places they visited in Jerusalem? Or Phoenicia? Athalia could expect no less from her younger daughter, who showed exceptional creativity and dedication to the gods. "Come on, Jothan," she prodded impatiently. "The suspense is killing me. Which temple?"

Jothan raised his dark brows and looked directly at Athalia, timing his statement for maximum effect. "The Temple of Jehovah."

Her audible gasp accompanied the jangle of bracelets as she raised her hand to her throat and fingered the gold necklace around her neck. "Oh, Jothan. She can't be seriously interested in such a man. Why haven't you put a stop it it? You know Jehovah worshipers are our strongest opposition!"

Jothan smiled wryly, his dark gaze penetrating hers. "Until they become Baal worshipers."

Athalia was thoughtful for a moment. She sipped her wine to calm the fear that had risen in her breast. "You do have a point," she said, then suddenly laughed, flashing a loving glance at Diblaim and grasping his arm. "The converts from Jehovah are often more enthusiastic than some who have grown up with Baalism."

"True, true, my dear." Diblaim reached over to pat her hand. "I tend to forget I was once an adherent of that religion. A very dull and boring time in my life." He attacked his food with a renewed vigor.

Athalia laughed delightedly; she took full credit for Diblaim's conversion. "I don't doubt for a moment that Gomer can handle such a situation properly."

Rizpah was staring at her husband. "You didn't tell me, Jothan, that Gomer had spoken to you about this."

Setting the goblet beside his plate, Jothan gazed at Rizpah with careful eyes. "My dear wife," he began, "you and I have had more important concerns to think about and discuss these past months, than your sister's interest in men."

Rizpah flinched at his response and looked down quickly at her plate. Jothan turned to Diblaim and began to speak of business matters.

The wind and rain subsided later that evening. Gomer heard sandaled feet approach, then stop in front of her curtained doorway. She waited until her name was called. Getting off the bed, she took a few steps toward the doorway. "Come in, Jothan," she said.

Jothan moved the curtain aside, bent his head and entered. For a moment his eyes lingered on the fine linen gown Gomer wore. The odor of perfumed oil filled the room. Servants had massaged her skin to a soft glow. Her long black hair had obviously been rubbed dry, for it spread out from her face in wild disarray. Looking around the room, his eyes lit upon the plate of untouched food.

"You were not hungry?"

"Not very." Her violet eyes searched his face questioningly, wondering why he had come.

"What's wrong, Gomer?" he asked gently.

Looking down, she shook her head.

"Are you—I mean, is everything all right?"

His voice held so much concern that she didn't understand at first. Then comprehension flooded her eyes as she looked up at him. Perhaps he thought the gods had blessed her with a child. But he had followed the method to prevent that. "I'm all right," she assured him. But her eyes were sad.

Jothan sighed with relief. "Then it must be your young man."

Her eyes filled with tears again and she bit her lower lip. "He's engaged to be married. He was angry when I told him I was married to the gods. He doesn't like me now." She wished she were at the temple. It would be easier to talk to him as her priest than as her brother-in-law.

"Angry?" Jothan questioned. "Has he seen you in anything other than that peasant girl's outfit you wear about the village?"

Gomer shook her head. "There was no occasion for it. I told him I was from the village. And who from the village goes about during the day wearing fine linens and silk? Or how many even have them? Anyway, I didn't want him to question me. He disapproves of our worship. I knew he would disapprove of me."

"But you told him?"

"I didn't mean to," she admitted. "But suddenly I wanted him to think I didn't care that he was engaged to be married. I didn't want to care. And then I suddenly no longer wanted him to think I was just another girl from the village."

Jothan was silent for a moment. "Some of the Jehovah worshipers disapprove of us because they don't understand, Gomer. Help him to understand. Bring him to the temple."

Gomer was about to say that Hosea would never go to the temple. But looking up into Jothan's face, she felt he knew something she did not. His lips smiled. He was older. He was wiser and had spent many years counseling persons with all sorts of problems. And she knew that many Jehovah worshipers became followers of Baal. Even her own father.

"After all," Jothan continued, his voice lower, "you are no longer Rizpah's little sister. You are Gomer, a woman in your own right and a temple goddess."

Jothan stepped back and grasped the curtains. To Gomer he seemed strangely tense and ill-humored. "Bring him to the temple," he repeated, then turned and left the room.

Gomer wondered if she were being foolish to give so much thought to a man who made it clear he did not approve of Baal worship and who admitted he was to be married. But then, why would he spend so many weeks, so many months of his time, just to tell her stories about his God?

She wondered what he would say if she told him that, more than liking his stories, she just liked to watch his handsome face; how the golden brown of his eyes turned from seriousness to playfulness; the excitement in them when he told his stories; the joy when he played with the children; the strange look she could not readily identify when he watched her sing for the children; when he called her "little dove" and "pretty dove"; and the sound of his deep, resonant voice as he spoke from the beautiful full lips she so wanted to touch with her fingertips. Would he care that she thought about him so much and so often?

Gomer sighed at her own irrationality when her thoughts

went so abruptly from joy to despair. It was not easy being a woman, not knowing things for certain. Surely he would not marry before the spring flowers appeared. And surely he would come to the well at the edge of the village at least once more.

She would pray. The gods had given a child to Rizpah and Jothan when they had almost decided Rizpah was barren. If they could do that, surely they could bring Hosea to her side. A new hope was kindled in her heart as she turned toward the small golden image of the wonderful goddess she worshiped.

Chapter Four

Days passed. Delicate petals breathed in the warmth of sunshine, then opened their umbrellas to expose God's rainbow of color. Springtime touched the hill country of Ephraim and the hearts of its inhabitants—with the exception of Hosea. He was unable to escape the infectious gloom of the previous rainy season. He could not see that sunshine had dispelled the gloom.

"You don't have to be so hard on yourself," Beeri told him, to which Hosea merely shrugged. Beeri would have rejoiced had his son wanted to work the fields with him, supervise the spring planting. But Hosea was not concerned with the crops. He was attempting to uproot something that had been planted deep within his being. Each morning Hosea rose with a problem he could not share with his parents. He sweated through the noonday heat and into the evening. He worked his muscles into exhaustion, sometimes to rise again without having changed his garments.

Three weeks passed. On Monday Hosea left the plow at noon and walked back to the house. His father remained in the fields; his mother stayed in the bakery. Hosea bathed, groomed himself, donned one of his finest brown robes with golden trim. From the bakery, Huldah could see him pacing restlessly about the courtyard.

"Are you going to see Marabah?" she called to him.

He shook his head, then strode off toward the brown hills.

Amazed at new life around him, and at dazzling sunlight against a blue sky, Hosea felt his heart grow lighter. He reprimanded himself for his foolishness. There was no reason not to go to the well again. In fact, there was every reason to go. Perhaps he could make one final attempt to reach the young girl before Baalism became an all-consuming part of her life.

Ignoring the uneasiness in the pit of his stomach, and the gnawing facts she had thrown at him, he felt he was being objective. He should not have left her bewildered by his angry countenance. She was not at fault. She could only believe what she had been taught.

Forcing his thoughts to happier days, he recalled when he had walked in the hills, then sat high above them, watching the gaiety of the children. He remembered how he and Gomer laughed together and spoke of the sunsets. Mostly, she had talked about the children and the humorous things they did. She could keep him laughing and interested in her stories. He learned of her love for music as well as her desire to write poetry and songs. Their times together had been a relief from his busy life of responsibilities, like fragrant flowers after a rain.

Gomer saw him as soon as he started down the hillside toward the well. Her heartbeat quickened and color rose to her cheeks. Her eyes did not leave him until he came to the well and sat beside her on the stones.

"I feared you would not come back," Gomer said softly. The light in her eyes said she was glad he came.

"I didn't think I would," Hosea replied quietly, looking out toward the landscape.

"Why did you?"

Hosea felt as if he were a person divided. One of the

persons—his deeper, innermost self—was saying silently, "I wanted to see you in your village-girl attire to assure myself that it was all a dream about your being part of the temple rituals." But he was not reassured, for today she was not wearing the short tunic. She was a young woman in a long gown of fine linen the color of the flax flowers. The soft pink reminded him of the touch of color in her cheeks. But he did not say that aloud.

Her black hair was not loose about her shoulders, but caught up in a thick twist, fastened with golden combs. Maybe, just maybe this was really what he wanted to see. He wondered if he really knew himself. Something inside was changing. The security he had always felt was shaken. Things were not as simple as he had always imagined. The world was not so easily separated into good and evil, right and wrong.

Hosea's other self replied out loud to her. "I felt it was wrong to leave you in anger. I have for almost a year talked with you and the children about my God. I have been His representative. But I think the last time we talked, I did not give a good impression of what God is like. I didn't want to leave you with that concept."

"What impression did you want to leave?" Gomer asked.

Hosea did not reply readily. When he spoke, his words were carefully chosen. "That He is good, and kind, and caring."

"But I think you are those things," she said quickly.

Hosea looked away. "I am sorry I was rude and abrupt with you."

"It's all right," she assured him. "I know you just don't understand."

"No," he contradicted, fighting to control that awful feeling threatening again to engulf him. "It was because I do understand."

Gomer said nothing. Hosea turned and looked at her for a long moment. Yes, she bore that same hurt expression. She was a sensitive girl who wanted his approval. "The children," he said in a low voice. "The ones you bring here. They are not simply from the village, are they?"

"Some are," she replied. "But most are children of the prophets of Baal. It is my duty to teach them forms of worship, dance and song. I did not tell you they were village children."

"No," he sighed. "I assumed." He knew within himself that he had wanted to assume.

Hosea looked out toward the landscape again. Gomer followed his eyes. "Look at that," she gestured with her graceful, slender hand. "That is what my god has done."

Hosea looked. The March winds had been chased away and the hillsides were tapestried with brilliant red, white, blue and cream anemones and delicate pink flowers. How sad, he thought, that she believed it was her god who did it.

"Have you been to one of our temples?" she asked carefully.

"It is forbidden," he answered abruptly.

"Oh, Hosea," she reprimanded. "How can you be so much against something you don't really know?"

"I have heard," he answered.

"And you base your conclusions on rumor?" she asked spiritedly, then without thinking touched his arm as if to prevent his becoming angry again and running away from her. His muscles tightened beneath her touch but he did not draw away.

Hosea found the temptation to enter the village of Bethel as inviting as passing through the gates of Sheol. He hadn't the slightest desire to see the temple of Baal. He wished he could whisk her away from it all. He wished she were tempted to come to his God. But what did she know of God? A few stories he had told to children. Could he induce her to go to the magnificent Temple in Jerusalem? But Jehovah did not want to be represented by the amount of gold in a structure, nor the ornamental objects there. God wanted to be represented by what was in the heart of man. The only way to show her Jehovah God was to show her a person of love.

A gasp of pleasure escaped her lips when Hosea stood, towered over her and smiled down at her. It did not matter so much that his eyes were sad. At least they were not angry when he consented, "All right. We will go to your temple."

The sun vanished behind tapestried hills, leaving a tranquil sky. The evening was warm. His face set straight ahead, Hosea nodded in answer to a question, or answered briefly. Only when they reached the village did he walk more leisurely and his face muscles relax, for village children played near their homes.

He and Gomer stopped to talk with them. He was easy with them and they loved him. How wonderful, she thought, if he would become part of their temple staff and teach the children. Perhaps they could teach them together.

"Look. You can see the temple from here." Gomer spoke proudly, looking up at the top of a hill. The sun had set. Dusk was closing in, but it was obvious how the temple would gleam in the sunlight, like a signal.

When they reached the bottom of the hill, Gomer pointed out her own residence. "It is temple property," she explained. "We live in it because my mother is High Priestess. She was a Phoenician princess."

Hosea looked at the house as they walked past. It was not as large as his parents' home but he recognized the Phoenician influence. The two-tiered structure was set against a hillside. A low wall surrounded a spacious outer court. Gomer explained that her mother and father no longer lived in the palace of their gods. "My sister, Rizpah, is married to the High

Priest. So they now live in the palace." Gomer did not notice his shudder as she continued to explain how perfect Jothan and Rizpah were together as they led the people in temple rituals.

Hosea stared intently at Gomer. "I suppose you get your violet eyes from your mother."

Gomer smiled. He hadn't said he liked them, but he had noticed. Everyone always commented about how unusual her eyes were and complimented her. "My mother's eyes are blue. So are Rizpah's."

"Your father's?"

"Brown. He's a Hebrew."

Hosea was surprised. "A Hebrew?"

Gomer nodded. "My father was already a goldsmith when he met my mother, and he often worshiped at the temple of Bethel when my mother came here. They fell in love almost immediately. Mother says"—she glanced toward him—"that Hebrew men are much more attractive than Phoenician." Hosea frowned.

How strange, she thought. Either he hadn't heard her or perhaps hadn't liked her to say that Hebrew men were attractive.

Darkness closed in as they ascended the hill, climbing the many steps to the top. She was unlike any woman he had ever known. There was a rare innocence and sweetness in her that so far had not been contaminated by her temple activities. She did not pretend to be delicate or offended by life and nature. Her grace and elegance probably came from her dancing, which she had told him was a daily necessity.

For a moment he rejoiced inwardly at her many abilities. Then he corrected himself. Her talents were used for the most abominable practices. He must not forget that.

Chapter Five

The temple of Baal stood majestically on the hilltop overlooking the village, where people at any time of day or night could look up and see where their gods dwelt. This too was of Phoenician architecture. Great cylindrical columns graced the entrance beneath the portico. Carved lions squatted at the base of the pillars.

"We will go in by a side entrance," Gomer said, taking his hand. "Those who aren't followers of Baal aren't allowed to enter from the main entrance or to look directly into the interior from the outside."

They walked around to the side. "It won't hurt to look," Gomer chided with a little laugh, noting Hosea's distraught expression.

He was not so certain. Sometimes one could look in a direction too long. He wondered if some of the priests of Jehovah had started this way, with a beautiful girl, whose countenance portrayed sweetness and innocence, luring them. *Will God be angry?* he wondered. But he stepped inside.

Young men in short tunics were lighting lamps placed in wall niches. A faint glow began to illuminate the spacious, rectangular, high-ceilinged room. As more lamps were lighted, a brilliance glittered on golden objects, shadows danced about the marble floor and elaborately carved ceiling. Around the room, against the walls, were benches for offerings.

The wide, gold, velvet-covered steps started in the center of the room. There were twenty of them on four sides, all leading to the huge golden figure on top of the raised dais. The idol had outstretched arms and a platter-like altar in front where sacrifices could be lain. Was this where Gomer's sister had placed her baby? In front of the idol was a long, low couch covered with red velvet.

The shadow-producing, flickering light quickened Hosea's imagination. He could almost see the dancers on the steps, on the couch, before the idol. He tried not to visualize the orgies he had heard took place on these steps. In younger days he had even found them exciting to think about. He did not realize he was staring at the sight before him until Gomer spoke.

"Do you dance, Hosea?"

Did Gomer dance on these steps? He did not look at her when he replied, but looked around the room. "We dance and sing to God in the Temple. King David had his own Temple staff of musicians, and that was a vital part of worship. He was very adept in the arts, as well as being a fierce warrior and leader of men. He wrote many of the songs we sing."

"Then you are not opposed to dancing," she said expectantly.

"Dancing before God Jehovah or at celebrations and festivals," he answered abruptly. "No, I am not opposed to that."

Gomer's face betrayed her disappointment. "Come over here," she entreated. "I want to show you something." They stepped over to one side. She took a wooden object from its nook in the wall and held it out to him. "This is my favorite goddess. Her name is Ashtoreth. Do you know about her?"

Hosea stared at the fertility goddess, naked, with a snake

draped around her neck and a lily in one hand, standing on a lion. Yes, he knew something about her.

"The people of Tyre and Sidon honor her," he said. "The Philistines paid homage to her and hung weapons of King Saul in her temple. Solomon raised a shrine to her." He looked at Gomer then and she stepped back at the fire in his eyes. "Josiah destroyed the shrine," he continued. "However, God's judgment was already passed. That is part of the reason the kingdom of Israel has been divided."

Gomer looked confidently down at the statue. "Ashtoreth was not destroyed. She is alive. She is Baal's wife. During the summer months, the sun is so hot and dry that death reigns supreme. Ashtoreth vanquishes death, for she is a warrior-goddess. She brings Baal back to life. Because of their mating, verdure covers the land in spring. As it does now," she explained, looking up at him. "Have you heard of her battles?"

"I have heard," he replied, and recalled the legend as Gomer set the idol back in its place. Ashtoreth, it was reported, had driven men into her temple and held them prisoners. By the time she had finished with them, she waded knee-deep in blood. The heads of her victims became ornaments around her neck and their hands were tied on a golden belt around her waist. Once she was satisfied, it was said that "her liver was swollen with laughter, and her heart full of joy."

"I have a gold statue of her at home," Gomer said, turning to face him. "My father made it for me to be presented when I wedded the gods." Her voice dropped in disappointment at the look on his face. "You are not impressed with our temple."

"Quite the contrary," he answered slowly, thoughtfully. But he was not happy with the impression he had. He began to understand how easy it would be to fall into the temptation of worshiping here, to delight in the stories of the gods and goddesses, to drink and dance and satisfy the physical and spiritual appetites, to forget God and think of the excitement of this kind of worship.

How many had been charmed by such as Gomer? Or by Gomer herself? He felt a sudden weakness in his knees, a great uneasiness. He was about to say he had seen enough when he noticed a figure appear at the back of the temple. There were steps all across the width of the room at the back. At the top of the steps was a floor off which were rooms at the sides and back. Multicolored curtains adorned the doorways.

The tall, dark-haired, bearded man in a black robe walked toward them. As he neared, Hosea realized the manner in which he carried himself gave an appearance of added height.

Gomer extended her hands to the man and smiled, her head back. "This is Jothan, the High Priest. Jothan, this is Hosea." She spoke with admiration and respect. Hosea decided she would feel about her High Priest the way he felt about his.

Letting go of her hands, Jothan turned to Hosea. "I'm glad you came," he welcomed him. His smile seemed forced, yet he was cordial. Hosea felt a growing tension between the two of them.

"Jothan is Rizpah's husband," Gomer reminded him. Hosea fought to control emotion that might show in his face. This would be the father of the sacrificed baby.

Jothan invited Hosea to return to the temple whenever possible, gave a parting smile to Gomer and walked back toward the curtained doorway. As Hosea and Gomer neared the exit, Hosea turned his head and looked back. Jothan had not gone back into the priest's room, but stood gazing intently in their direction. Then he raised his hand in a parting gesture, and quickly turned toward the priest's room.

Hosea wondered briefly at the expression on Jothan's face. He sensed hostility, but the look was cordial. Perhaps it was his imagination, for he had expected to find something gory and evil here. The priests of Jehovah in the Temple at Jerusalem would not have been so friendly to Jothan.

The fragrance of the gardens greeted them as they stepped outside the temple and into the groves. "Some services are held here, aren't they?" Hosea asked.

"Yes. Would you like to see one?"

His answer was quick. "I may have already offended God by going into the temple."

"Where is your God? Do you have an image of Him?"

"He forbids an image," Hosea explained. "He is here, there, everywhere."

Gomer did not even pretend to understand. "If you can't see Him, touch Him, how can you worship Him?"

His retort was sharp. "If you can make a god, he is not a god at all."

"These are symbols, Hosea. Surely you have symbols. Show me your God."

Show her my God? Hosea thought. *How can I do that—an invisible God who lives within? She knows what her gods look like, for she has statues. They have names.*

"These gods are not just objects," Gomer continued when he did not answer. "Much power comes from them."

Hosea was sure of that. But she was not aware of the source of that power.

Gomer challenged him with her eyes. "Many who believe in Jehovah still come to our temple and worship."

Hosea's dark eyes flashed. "I know. But it is against the teachings of Jehovah. They are wrong. That is not God's way."

"It is my god's way." She lifted her head proudly and the moonlight bathed her lovely face. After a moment of silence Gomer asked in a low voice, "When are you planning to marry?"

Hosea could have answered that he had planned it for most of his twenty-four years. He was one of the few men still single at his age. And yet it was not he who had planned it. It had been arranged for him. "The plans for my wedding are to be discussed this week. My major priestly studies have ended and this seems an ideal time. It has been decided that I must marry."

"Must?" Her eyes searched his.

"I mean, I . . . we . . . have planned."

"Oh," she said, and for a moment looked around at the darkened garden with patches of moonlight shining through the branches of trees. When she looked at him again, her eyes were large and sad. "You will not come and talk to me anymore."

Hosea's heart softened. Not ever see the little girl-woman he had known for a year? "Of course I'll come and talk with you, little dove."

Gomer smiled at the name.

Then she shook her head. "She won't let you."

"She?"

"Your wife. She will not like me."

Hosea stared at her. No. Marabah would not like her. "What about you?" he asked suddenly. "Do you want to marry? Have children? Or is that forbidden to you?"

"I can do as I please. It is recommended that I marry now. First I had to be married to the gods since I come from a line of High Priestesses, and it appeared that Rizpah might be barren, which meant I would have taken her place as the temple High Priestess."

Taking a deep breath that squared his shoulders, Hosea fought back the rage that was beginning to take hold in his chest. There were things he must know. "Your husband would not mind that you . . . marry with the gods, as you call it?"

Gomer stared at him. "But he should understand that I have been honored."

"Are your rituals in a group?" Hosea probed.

"Some are," she replied. "But I'm not that privileged yet. I'm just in training. I've had only one partner."

His eyes were glued to her face. "Partner?" he spat.

Defiance flashed in her eyes. "Yes. Jothan," she replied stubbornly.

"Ah!" Hosea gasped and lifted his hand to his brow and turned his face toward the moonlight. Jothan. The High Priest. The father of the sacrificed baby. Her sister's husband. The man who had looked at him with resentment he could not quite conceal. Now he understood that expression on Jothan's face. It was not because he had entered a sacred temple; it was because he was with Gomer.

Like a cold winter's blast, it struck his heart. There was talk that Baal-worshiping women were of loose morals, wayward women. The icy cold was melting into anger. He wanted to scream out to Gomer. If he did not get away he would surely allow his anger to turn into bitter rage.

"I must go," he said suddenly. "Something I must do. You understand?"

Gomer understood all too well. Reaching up, she touched his handsome face. A sob was in her whisper. "I don't condemn you for your kind of worship. I wish you did not—" Her voice broke. Standing on tiptoes, she lifted her face to his and kissed him gently on the lips.

"Be happy," she whispered and pulled away when he made no response. Turning, she ran through an entrance and into the temple, the tears spilling over onto her cheeks.

Hearing his own raspy breath, Hosea asked himself why a man of God was standing in Baal's shady groves, his insides on fire, threatening to melt away all reason. With a cry, he strode from the temple gardens, away from Gomer, away from the pagan temple, down the hill, through the village, past the well and into the wooded hills. He felt that his heart would beat out of his chest. There was a deep hurting inside and he did not think it was from striding.

"Please, God," he said aloud. "Take this temptation from me. That must surely be what it is—the powers of darkness trying to take my soul from You and involve me in these pagan rites. I am tempted, God, just to be with this beautiful woman. There is a part of her that is the little girl who laughs and sings. I want to be with her, too. Not in ugliness, Lord, but in beauty. I should think of my future wife, but I think of the one forbidden to me. Please take this feeling from me, God. Make me whole and clean and pure, so that I can be Your priest, the kind of son my parents want, the husband Marabah deserves. I am not good enough. I am not strong enough. Use someone better than I to be Your priest, O God, but do not abandon me. Please remove this burden. Please remove my hatred for the pagan priest who would touch her. My life is filled with hatred, anger, and desire for a pagan woman, an idolater. Please God, if You ever heard me, hear me now."

Hosea struck a tree with the side of his fist, and lowered his tear-stained face toward the ground.

Chapter Six

Marabah sat up suddenly as if a spring had snapped, jerking her upper body forward. She knew who it was as soon as the distant figure emerged from the thicket beyond the village. Hosea! He should not be coming this way, for tonight was when their families were to meet for finalizing wedding plans. He should be home, getting ready.

A tightness seized her chest as she rose from the couch on the roof of her parents' home where she had dozed in the midafternoon sun. Only moments before, Marabah's eyes had wandered toward that wooded area, just beyond which Hosea had built a house for her and the children they would someday have. She had dreamed of Hosea's strong arms around her, his coming home at evening in his priestly garb, her keeping the house, tending the children, entertaining important guests.

Attempting to eradicate the sudden dread that settled about her, Marabah rose from the couch and walked down to the second floor to her bedroom. She smoothed the soft material of her dress over the full figure of which she was proud, then drew herself up to her full height, which was a shade over average, but complimented Hosea's tall, muscular frame. She was a sturdy woman, large-boned but feminine. The stiff bristles of the brush and the afternoon sunshine had worked their magic in leaving a glowing auburn sheen to her dark brown hair that fell softly to her shoulders.

Why was she so uneasy? Then she reprimanded herself. He could be coming into the village for any number of reasons. She tried not to think about the times he had come to postpone the wedding, saying he wanted to build a house for her, that he wanted to accumulate more wealth for the family he would have, that he wanted to complete his studies. No amount of protest on her part had made a dent in his stubborn ways. But now that was behind them. With lifted chin, she again looked at her reflection and spread her full mouth into a smile over straight white teeth. She knew that her smile was one of her best features, yet her large brown eyes were full of apprehension.

She heard her mother greeting Hosea in the inner court. "Are you looking for Asa, or would you like to see . . . Marabah?"

Marabah drew in her breath at Hosea's reply. "I would like to see Marabah, please." She knew suddenly that this visit was not because he couldn't bear to be away from her.

"I'm right here, Mother," Marabah said, walking regally into the small courtyard, pasting a warm smile across her face and holding out her hands toward her betrothed. "Hosea," she said, "what are you doing here?"

She had come to know and dread that stubborn set of his jawline, the shielded eyes beneath a furrowed brow that always brought with it a tale of woe. But she would pretend. She'd had much practice at that. Her face lifted for his kiss on each cheek.

"You look lovely, Marabah," Hosea said, his eyes taking in the sun-touched young woman who had draped a white lacy shawl about her shoulders.

Marabah lowered her eyes. Lovely? But that was not

enough. What did Hosea want? Why was he here, when they were to meet only hours from now to plan the wedding?

"I have to talk to you, Marabah."

Marabah nodded, lifted her chin though her spirit was sinking. "We can walk," she said. They left the courtyard and strolled along the dusty village street.

Deborah stood at the entrance of the courtyard, looking after her daughter and Hosea as the young couple walked up the village street. Several neighbors were outside—talking, beginning their spring cleaning, preparing gardens, and generally enjoying the warm sunshine. Deborah loved the village. She and her husband, Asa, were the first settlers here and had made it their home for almost thirty-five years. It had been a good place to rear their five children.

Her thoughts drifted back to the years when Asa and Beeri had bought land in the country a dozen miles from Jerusalem. The two young couples in time had built homes and moved there. A small village had grown around them. Asa's efforts, however, had not prospered like Beeri's. Then, when a fall from a horse left him with a permanent limp preventing him from working the fields, he had sold his land to Beeri. Beeri then had asked Asa to be his business manager. Soon it had become a permanent arrangement.

Asa had never regretted that arrangement, for it had brought him contact with businessmen and priests, many of whom had become friends, and he was blessed with more than land and wealth. He had man's greatest pride: children to carry on his name. Four boys, then Marabah. Hosea had been born to Huldah and Beeri only a few months before Marabah came. While the babies were still in their mothers' wombs, there was talk of their being promised to each other if one was a boy and the other a girl.

Determined not to waste time with her thoughts, Deborah went inside the house to the sewing room to continue stitching the golden braid on Marabah's white wedding gown. There was no dinner to prepare since they would dine with Beeri and Huldah. She would wait just a little longer before dressing for the evening.

She laid the garment aside when Asa came into the house shouting her name. He hugged her as she came to the doorway, then quickly related the day's experience of looking over their property. "I think we should add it to Marabah's dowry. After all, you and I will have this entire house to ourselves. It's more than adequate, don't you agree?"

"You know I agree, Asa," Deborah replied, her small oval eyes looking at him warmly.

Asa dropped his hands and wiped perspiration from his receding hairline and down across his long, coarse beard. "I will tell Beeri tonight," he added, nodding, as Deborah smiled at him. Then she looked away. They both knew that it would not matter to Huldah, Beeri or Hosea whether or not Marabah even had a dowry.

Marabah and Hosea walked in silence for a while. "Marabah," he began, clearing his throat, "I do not think I am going to become a priest."

Stopping in her tracks, Marabah stared at him. "But that is your life. You've always planned to be a priest. All you have to do is to take your vows, Hosea."

"I cannot take my vows when I have come to hold so much of the priesthood in contempt. Half of them have abandoned the Lord God Jehovah already. They make a sham of religion."

"We've talked about this before, Hosea," Marabah said impatiently. "You have always spoken of how much you want to join those who have not turned away from Jehovah. And think of your influence when you become a priest."

Hosea shook his head, walking on toward the trees beyond the village. "At this time, I simply cannot."

"Then what will you do?" she almost snapped.

Hosea shrugged his broad shoulders. "I don't know. I suppose I will work the fields with my father until I know. Until God reveals what He wants me to do."

Marabah watched as he leaned back against a tree, not meeting her eyes. Her voice was strained. "And you feel you must postpone the wedding until God reveals some vocation to you."

"I'm sorry," he began.

"Sorry?" Her voice rose. "And when do you suppose God will reveal his plan, Hosea? In a few days? Is God going to call you into something you haven't prepared for? Has He led you into the priesthood to have you throw it all away? Is this a postponement"—she gasped for breath—"indefinitely?"

He turned away from her and lifted his face toward the treetops. "I'm not sure that God wants me to marry."

So it was said. This was not a postponement. It was final. There would be no wedding. The silence was interminable. Finally he turned to look at Marabah's face. Her jaw was set in a stubborn way and her eyes seemed glazed. Her lips trembled slightly. He felt miserable, hurting her this way.

"Maybe I'm wrong," he ventured further. "But it isn't fair to either of us if I'm not sure. You understand that, don't you, Marabah?"

Marabah's eyes blazed. She lifted her head higher. "This is God's will? Or just yours?"

With troubled eyes, he reached for her. "Marabah," he said softly, "try to understand."

Stepping back, she almost lost her balance avoiding his hand. "Why is God letting this happen to me?" she lashed out. "Does He not want me to marry? Did He want me to wait all these years so I could be humiliated? Only to be told I'm not wanted?" Her voice kept rising. "Don't you know that most of my friends have been married for years? Have children?"

Hosea stared beyond her, hearing her words, hating himself for what he was doing. He thought of the house he had built for her—the one they had planned together. It was finished now but he had not lived in it. It had been a source of pride to Marabah, being the most spacious dwelling around, other than his father's home. It was on the outskirts of the village in a wooded area, at the edge of the brown hills.

He could not blame God for the face of the girl who always seemed to be in his mind. But how could he marry Marabah, feeling he must do everything possible to save another woman from the pagan idolatry that could destroy her? How could he lie with Marabah, knowing he preferred a beautiful temple priestess who, though abominable to his spiritual nature, was an irresistible temptation to the physical and emotional part of him?

Always she was between him and thoughts of Marabah. She with the raven hair, the large fun-filled violet eyes so full of life and excitement who had placed her lips to his. He had not responded outwardly, for he had been promised to Marabah. She knew he was promised, yet still beckoned him to come to her, talk with her, be with her. No, he could not blame God for such a thing.

"I should not have said it was God," Hosea admitted to Marabah. "The fault lies within myself."

"I don't really blame God, either, Hosea," Marabah added penitently. "I know if it's the way you feel, you must say it. I'm sure you have struggled with such a decision, and I don't think you have deliberately tried to hurt me. But, Hosea, I want to marry. I want children. And I've waited so many years for you. What do I do now? Spend my life unmarried? Caring for other people's children? Become some man's second wife?"

"It won't be like that, Marabah." He was as distressed as she. "Any man would be fortunate to have you for a wife."

"Any man?" she replied bitterly.

"The fault is not in you, Marabah. It is within me."

She nodded. "All right. I'll accept that. Now, all I have to do is find that man. Perhaps Father will double my dowry. Perhaps there is a poor young man somewhere who can be bribed into marrying an old woman of twenty-four."

Turning, she began to walk very fast toward her home. Hosea walked with her. "No," she gasped. "Don't come with me. Please."

Hosea stopped. Marabah walked regally for a distance. Curious glances followed her and came back to rest on Hosea. They would be wondering why she walked so fast and now began to run, placing her hands over her face.

Hosea's heart hurt for her, while at the same time he felt a great burden lifted from him. He consoled himself with the fact that it would have been a greater hurt to marry her. She deserved better.

No one would understand. He did not understand. He just knew he could not marry Marabah. Not now, not ever. He could not even say it was the will of God. He no longer knew the will of God. Perhaps, indeed, God did not want him to marry. He walked slowly toward his father's home.

Hosea paused at the doorway of the kitchen. His mother was preparing dinner for the expected guests of the evening. His father was savoring the aroma of the food. They both looked toward the doorway where Hosea stood. "Sit down, son," Beeri said. "You look tired."

"I have to talk to you," Hosea said for the second time that day. Again he had to hurt those he loved, and he wished there were another way.

Huldah wiped her hands on her apron, and the three sat down at the kitchen table.

"I cannot marry her."

"What?" Beeri stammered.

Huldah's face grew pale.

Hosea repeated slowly, "I cannot marry Marabah."

"What do you mean, you cannot marry Marabah? You've had a quarrel," his mother soothed. "That is nothing. It will pass."

"No quarrel," he said, and added as an afterthought, "I don't think we've ever really quarreled."

Huldah shook her head in bewilderment. She knew her son had postponed the wedding several times, but attributed that to level-headedness, not reluctance. "What is it, Hosea?"

He stood up and turned from them. "I don't know, exactly. I just can't marry her. That's all."

"Does she displease you in some way, Hosea?" Huldah asked.

"No, Mother," Hosea could answer honestly. "I find no fault with Marabah. None at all."

Beeri stared at his son numbly. "You know this has been planned for years, Hosea. Why this sudden change of mind?"

"I'm not sure it's sudden, Father." Hosea faced them both. "I always thought I would marry her eventually. But I kept putting it off. I can't put it off any longer and I can't go through with it."

"Hosea," Huldah pleaded, "how can you do this? Deborah

and Asa are coming tonight to make plans. Does Marabah know?"

"I told her this afternoon."

"Oh, Hosea. The poor girl."

"It's better this way, Mother. Maybe God doesn't want me to marry."

Beeri frowned as he watched Hosea closely. "Do you believe God does not want you to marry, Hosea?"

"I cannot truthfully say what God's will is, Father. I wish I could."

"Is there someone else you want to marry?"

"No," Hosea snapped. His reply was quick. Too quick. "Nothing like that," he said defensively. "I'm sorry I have disappointed you, Father. Mother. I'm sorry for the distress I have caused Marabah and her family." Hosea's eyes pleaded for them to understand what even he could not understand, but theirs reflected only confusion.

"I'm sorry," he said again, then walked out the door.

Hosea returned late. He went to the private room set aside for studying the Scriptures, worshiping and praying. His mother and father were there, kneeling, their backs to him. He placed his hands on their shoulders. They turned, stood and faced him with tears in their eyes.

"We felt you needed our prayers especially tonight, Hosea," Huldah said in broken tones. "We pray that you will see the error of your ways and return to Marabah."

"I want you to pray for me, Mother. And you, Father. And I want to do what the Lord wants me to do."

Beeri and Huldah left the room, their hearts heavy for their son. They had never known him to be so distressed.

Chapter Seven

Gomer had felt sad ever since the night at the temple when she touched Hosea's lips with her own. But he had stood like a statue, not responding, not touching her. She had gone into the temple and stood with her back against the wall, letting the tears run down her cheeks. His lips were for another woman, his arms for someone else. She should not care. Everything in her life had been beautiful and exciting—until she met Hosea.

He was the only discordant note in her life and she told herself she would be better off without him. No one else had ever made her cry like this. No one else had made her consider questioning her beliefs. She should forget him. She had a career. She was beautiful. She was a goddess.

"I won't care," she said aloud. "I will forget him. I will be happy again."

Jothan came and wiped away the tears. "You should not cry," he chided gently. "I have told you how difficult it is for Hebrews to understand us. But his coming here tonight was a major victory for you."

Gomer's sad eyes looked at him through wet lashes. "But he's going to marry a—a Hebrew woman." The tears started again.

"Would you be content for him to come here and worship if he were married?"

"Oh, no," she admitted, shaking her head. "I want to be with him all the time. When he leaves me, my heart goes with him. I always thought if I cared for someone so much, he would have to feel the same way. I didn't know it would be so painful, that anything could hurt so much."

Jothan lifted her quivering chin with his fingertips. His voice was filled with concern. "Don't you know it is against everything a devout Hebrew holds sacred for him to come to this temple?"

She looked up at him and he dropped his hand to his side. She remembered that Hosea had said that. Seeing he had her attention, Jothan added, "Ask yourself why he becomes angry with you. Is it not because he cares?"

"I know that he cares, but not in the way he cares for the children. He does not even hold my hand, unless I reach for his."

"That, too, is typical of a devout Hebrew," Jothan assured her. "Hebrew men also think that restraint outside of marriage is a part of their God's law. To him, this indicates an even greater caring for you—a respect."

"How can he think like that?" she asked, amazed.

Jothan shrugged. "It is a part of their teaching from early childhood."

"Then," she said, a small light in her eyes, "he would keep himself from the Hebrew woman he's engaged to."

"Don't you think," Jothan said pointedly, "that if he did not have such restraint, he would be with her on Monday nights, instead of with you?"

Gomer shook her head slightly. "It's all so confusing."

Jothan nodded. "That's because it's a matter of the heart. The heart never listens to the head, unfortunately. But you must have faith in our gods."

She nodded and he added, "Let us offer a sacrifice." Taking her arm, he led her up the gold-carpeted steps toward the great golden god above them.

A faint smile crossed her lips. A new hope was aroused. She should trust her gods to return him to her. She would have faith.

Later that night, lying in her bed, Gomer thought of Jothan's words. She was less emotional now and Jothan's words had seemed to make sense. She recalled his talking about sexual restraint on the part of Hebrews. She could understand that. Her own temple rules and family rules were also very strict. They were carefully instructed in sexual behavior and the restraint was necessary to avoid unwanted pregnancies.

Sex in the temple was quite different, of course, and done in tribute to their gods. The staff often began their sexual activity as early as fourteen or fifteen years of age, but it was widely accepted among the followers of Baal that these people were the sacred temple staff and that it was a high honor to serve their gods with one's body.

Her own sexual activity had been delayed since she was of the priestly line and to be mated only with a High Priest or important temple assistant. It was something she had never questioned, but accepted and anticipated with great delight.

Surely, if Hosea really understood, he could not object to the beautiful ceremony in which she had been wedded to the gods. She turned her head now to look at the golden statue of Ashtoreth. Her mind drifted back to the evening Jothan had given the statue to her.

"This is the goddess you will represent," he had said, handing her the statue. "Your father made it for this occasion."

She looked at it with admiration; then Jothan took it and

placed it on the low table in the corner that was between two scarlet-colored couches.

They were in Jothan's private chambers where no one was allowed without the invitation of the High Priest. The only light was from the soft glow of two candles on each side of the huge god at the far end of the room. In front of the god was a low, long and wide couch, made of gold. Attached at the top of the four golden, intricately carved poles was an embroidered white and gold canopy with gold fringe. Veils of fine silk, scarlet, gold and white were pulled back, revealing the thick white padding of the couch, covered with fine linen. The circular carpet on which the couch sat was like that on the steps in the outer room.

Her eyes had wandered about the room in admiration of its beauty. She and Jothan sipped wine and spoke of the ceremony to follow. It was orderly and unemotional at first. She felt comfortable with him. He said it was important to be in a meditative frame of mind, so she allowed the wine, the fragrance of incense, and the music that was being played on the landing outside the private chamber to become part of her being. She smiled at Jothan when they had finished the wine and set the goblets down. He lifted her hand as they began to dance.

She knew the steps. She had a natural talent for dancing, as well as years of instruction. Every day for the past week she had practiced the dance steps with Beniah, while Jothan watched. She had felt a reticence with Beniah. Jothan must have sensed it, for he suggested that he would be her partner during the ceremony instead of Beniah. She was glad.

When the dance began Gomer was aware that she was an inexperienced girl and he a mature older man. But as she danced around the couch, then returned to him and they swayed to the music in front of the god, and he told her of her beauty and grace, her mind and body relaxed.

He kept reminding her that he was Baal and she was Ashtoreth. She did not know if it was the wine or the excitement of the ceremony or all of it, but the exact steps were forgotten as she and Jothan danced closer and closer before the gods. She felt herself being kissed on her face and neck and shoulders. No one had adequately described how the sweet glow inside became a flickering flame and then an all-consuming fire. No one had said how the body would come alive and crave a satiating for the sweet desire.

She knew what to expect when he led her to the couch. She welcomed the slight pain that passed as soon as it came and reveled in the ecstasy she had known would follow, for it was the moment she changed from being a child into a woman, and then a goddess. She was Ashtoreth and he was Baal and it was a more wonderful experience than anyone had ever told her.

She had cried because of the beauty and awesomeness of moving away from the realm of childhood into womanhood. She would have liked to have held her god close for a time afterward, but she knew his withdrawal from her was for the purpose of spilling his seed into the sacred vessel that he would offer as the final sacrifice of the ceremony. It was not the kind of ceremony where the god would find his own pleasure, but a time of teaching a goddess how to submit and find her own fulfillment.

It was the sacred duty of the High Priest to keep the goddess from becoming pregnant unless she consented to it. There would be other private ceremonies before she would be considered ready for the public ritual. And when it was the right time of the moon for her, they could find their pleasure together. She could not imagine how she could ever feel more complete and at peace with herself and her gods than she did at that moment.

Now, as she lay in her own bed, remembering, and again felt the wetness on her face, she did not know how anyone could cry so much. She wished that Hosea could believe Jothan was a god, and that her way of worship was a sacred duty, but her private life separate. And Hosea, whether or not he ever became a part of temple life, was the one she wanted in her private life.

Gomer continued to go to the well several days out of each week in hopes of meeting Hosea. A younger girl was with her now and would soon take Gomer's place with the young children. Gomer would become a teacher for older girls, instructing them in dance, art, personal grooming, make-up, temple rules and sacred duties.

The rains had ceased and the world was alive with the beauty of spring. The sky was virtually cloudless. It was a time to be enjoyed, for the droughts and intense heat would soon set in.

There were several times, playing with the children at the well, that she thought Hosea stood on the hillside looking down at them. Perhaps it was just her wishful thinking, but she was almost sure she caught a glimpse of him. On Monday evenings when she came alone, she felt as if he were near, but he did not come to her and she was saddened.

Three weeks passed and he did not return to talk to her.

"The sacrifice did no good," she said to Jothan. "I thought I could bear it, but I cannot. I know he is there in the hills, but he does not come to me."

"We will talk in my private chambers," Jothan suggested.

They reclined on the low scarlet couches in the semi-darkness in the corner of the room and sipped wine from golden goblets. The wine, incense and Jothan's voice combined to make a consoling effect.

"Beniah wants to marry you," Jothan said at one point.

Gomer's eyes widened. "He said that?"

Jothan nodded and Gomer protested, "I don't even like Beniah."

Jothan's dark eyes studied his young pupil. "Why don't you like him?"

Gomer shrugged. "Maybe his eyes are too close together."

"Gomer," Jothan chided, "you know that isn't true."

"Well," she said coyly, "they are closer than anyone else's I know." Thinking about him, which she preferred not to do, she supposed his appearance was rather striking, typical of the men chosen to lead in the temple. He was tall and dark, in his mid-twenties.

But there was something unnerving about the way his black eyes narrowed when he looked at her, making his fine-lined brows rise to peaked arches. He had a way of clenching and unclenching his hands that annoyed her. When she ignored him, his lips set in a straight line like some pouting child's. And she didn't like his beard. It was coal-black and straight, like his hair. Everyone said he was handsome, but she supposed, like her mother, she found Hebrew men much more attractive.

"Actually, Jothan," she continued seriously, "it's something in the way he looks at me. And all he ever talks about is money."

Jothan laughed. "That is in his favor. After all, he is our temple treasurer. And as you know, you are supposed to be his partner in the public services. Of course, he has looked forward to that, feeling as he does about you."

A shudder ran through her. Then her eyes brightened. "But if Hosea joins us. . . ."

Jothan smiled and nodded. "Then he would be your partner without question."

"Make it happen, Jothan." She reached across to lay her hand on his.

Jothan concentrated on his wine goblet. "We will arrange for the next private ceremony to be held Monday evening."

She withdrew her hand. "But Hosea and I always met on Mondays. If he came, it would be on Monday evening."

"Trust me," Jothan said and stood, which she felt was a dismissal. She left the chambers. Of course she would trust him. He was her High Priest.

Jothan sat for a while after she had gone, sipping his wine. An inner concern faintly marred the expectancy of the ceremony he would plan. He truly hoped the gods would grant her wish and bring Hosea to her, that he might take part in the temple rituals. For Gomer, just past eighteen, little more than a child, had seemed that one unforgettable night to be Ashtoreth herself, with the power of life and death in her hands. She was truly a perfect goddess, dedicated, ardent, lovely. She was almost a conquering goddess who might even subdue her mate, the great, all-powerful Baal.

Chapter Eight

Several times Hosea thought of talking with his father about Gomer and yet he hesitated. What advice could his father give him, except to urge him to stay away from her?

He thought of going to Jerusalem and discussing it with Jason. Jason was ten years older than he, and as a rabbi and priest had taught him much of what he knew about the Scriptures. They had, over the past few years, become close friends and talked often about the decaying political status of Judah and the threat of Egypt. They spoke of the rise of Assyria to the north. He and Jason both were concerned with the outward appearance of Israel's prosperity, while many political, social, economic and religious injustices prevailed. There was an internal decay taking place throughout Israel as people turned toward pseudo-prosperity and away from God who had led them into the land. There was increasing violence and oppression of the poor.

Those things he could discuss with his friend, but he did not think Jason could help in the matter of Gomer. He knew the laws. He knew God's instructions concerning idol worshipers. What advice could anyone give that he was not already aware of?

Hosea prayed earnestly day after day, fasted and meditated, but found no release from his thoughts of the lovely girl caught in the vices of Baalism. He saw her from a distance as she played with the children at the well. He knew when she was at their meeting place on Monday night but would not approach her. He determined not to speak with her again. He would find another place for his meditation, where he and Gomer had not walked and talked.

But this was the fourth Monday night since their encounter at the temple and she was not here. Perhaps she would not come again. If she did not, then his problem would be solved. Wouldn't it?

But not seeing her there suddenly became more unbearable than seeing her. A thought kept running through his mind: *My pretty dove is in the hands of vultures.*

"What can I do?" he wailed to God aloud. He could not continue to see her without a chance of succumbing to her tempting invitation. He could not spend his life trying to avoid her. What then?

He could find no peace.

"What do You want me to do?" he asked aloud. "Why don't You answer me, God?" He was desperate and angry, and lifted his face toward heaven where the silver stars twinkled against a deep blue background. His fists were doubled and the nails dug into his palms. "Why don't You take this from me? Do You want me to marry her?"

Marry her! Hosea was frightened by the thought. It was out of the question. Such a thought could not be from God. A priest of Jehovah could not, by law, marry a pagan woman. But he had already decided he would not take his priestly vows.

But such a thing was still strictly forbidden by God. That was one reason the kingdom of Israel was divided. Solomon's pagan wives, for whom he built altars for their idols, had been his downfall. Such a thought must have come to Hosea from Sheol.

Yet his thoughts were not wicked. His feelings for her were not lust, but dwelt on her sweetness and gentle spirit. He cared very much about what happened to her eternal soul. He did not want to worship as she did. He did not want a false god. Was there no way to turn her from the idols, from the activity that could bring only sorrow and degradation?

Suddenly there was a stillness. Never had he felt such silence. The forest was still. Not a leaf waved in a breeze. There was no breeze. Not an insect made a sound. He listened. The world seemed insensate.

"God, do You want me to marry her?" he asked in a quiet voice. Suddenly his heart beat wildly and a burden lifted from his shoulders. He breathed more easily and was astounded.

God had spoken to him!

His heart and mind echoed the two words: *Marry her.*

How strange the feeling he now had! What was it? Then he knew. It was something he hadn't had in many months since his caring for Gomer had started, grown and overtaken him. It was—peace.

Was it from God? It had to be. God knew somehow that Gomer would abandon her idols. God was wiser than he.

It was as if time stood still and in that interminable silence all of Israel paraded before his mind. God did not abandon Israel when she worshiped false gods. He warned against it. He led His chosen people out of slavery and degradation into a fertile land. He did not destroy His people, but He guarded them, taught them, loved them.

"I love her," Hosea said aloud. "As God loves Israel, I love Gomer."

He lifted his arms toward the sky, turned his face toward heaven but could not give a shout of praise. As quickly as he had grasped the answer, he now felt the doubt. He must not accept this unquestionably. He must not blindly believe that such a thought would come from God. It could be a trick of the evil forces to involve him in forbidden pagan practices.

Then he recalled that Gomer's sister was married to the High Priest. If Gomer were allowed to marry, perhaps she could only marry someone connected with the temple. Her parents would never allow her to marry a Hebrew. But her mother had married a Hebrew. Certainly they would not allow her to marry a Jehovah worshiper. He began to accept the impossibility of marriage with her.

Aside from that, suppose he took her in his arms. He would remember that the High Priest had done the same. He would kiss her lips and see the sneer about Jothan's mouth. He would look upon her beauty and see Jothan's eyes. He would think of Jothan's hands as he touched her. God would bring this remembrance to turn him from Gomer once and for all. He could not marry someone whom he could not bear to touch.

There were so many reasons why such a marriage could never be. Perhaps that was the reason for the sense of peace. He now knew what he would do. He would see her again and tell her that he could never become involved in her kind of worship. He would take her in his arms and discover how impossible it was to love her, knowing she had already been touched by another man. Yes, this was the beginning of his acceptance that the relationship had nowhere to go. They would both accept the fact that they could never see each other again, no matter how much it hurt.

As Hosea walked to their meeting place the following Monday, he thought perhaps she would not be there. Perhaps she had decided never to come again. But when he climbed the cliff he saw her sitting on the rocky ledge, her feet drawn up beside her. The fading sun lay gently on her smooth, tanned shoulders. Her dress was of pale blue, an exquisitely fine material. Her dark hair was caught up in a twist and fastened with jeweled combs.

When Hosea approached, she lifted her head slightly and turned her eyes toward him. He saw the light that came into them. How foolish, he thought, to think of Gomer in terms of other temple goddesses, as a wayward woman. She was but a child, really.

Hosea held out his hand. Gomer placed hers in his with a sweet shyness and stood before him, her gaze one of adoration. He looked away from it and led her along the path into the hills, where they often walked. They walked in silence.

He said something about the sunset being beautiful. Gomer agreed. Soon they came to a small clearing where they could look out onto the hills and valley below them. The fading sun was leaving behind a blushing sky.

Afraid he might be making the greatest mistake of his life, Hosea stopped and turned her to face him. Now is when he would see Jothan. He took her in his arms and brought his lips down upon hers. With a little moan she closed her eyes and lifted her arms around his neck. Hosea felt her body press against his and her heart beat against his chest. Jothan was not there at all, only his own lips, his own hands as they pressed her closer to himself, only his own eyes when he finally drew back from her. Her lips were parted in breathless surprise. A look of joy filled her eyes. Anticipation was in her expression. Now the words he must say.

"My sweet dove," he said, breathless from the wild beating of his heart. "I love you. We must marry soon."

"Oh," Gomer gasped, and quick tears sprang to her eyes. "I

didn't think—I mean—oh, Hosea. I didn't think you cared about me so much. Marry?"

"You will?" He was astounded. But he had asked.

"Oh, yes." She rushed into his arms, lifting her mouth to his. "I love you," she breathed against his lips. "Oh, I love you so much."

"Oh, my sweet dove. My love." With effort, Hosea finally broke away and moved back from her. The wild surging of emotion that had engulfed them threatened to eliminate all reason, all restraint.

"Why do you push me away?" she questioned.

Hosea's emotions were in turmoil. He knew that Gomer had been taught to be giving, loving, tender, and to please the gods with her body. If she would please the gods, she would please the man she loved. But his beliefs were different. He could not let himself succumb to his desires.

"I am not a Hebrew woman," she reminded him.

How aware of that he was! He would not have kissed a Hebrew woman like that, nor would she have allowed it, not unless—

With difficulty, Hosea reminded himself, as well as her, "But I am a Hebrew man."

Hosea knew that Gomer was surprised at his restraint. He hoped she did not know that he was not nearly as strong as he forced his voice to sound. Reaching out, he placed his hand on a tree to steady the trembling in his body.

With a graceful, dancelike step Gomer hugged her arms to herself and lifted her face toward the rose-deepened sky. Her laugh was a light, musical sound.

"What is humorous?" He walked over to her.

"You are." She stood on tiptoes to brush her lips across his. "But I love you, so very much."

His arms enfolded her and tightened, but his lips were now set in a firm line.

"When?" she asked, looking into his face.

"Soon," he said, drawing her near, caressing her hair as he held her head close to his chest. With eyes almost free of doubt, he watched the fading light disappear and a darkness settle about the hills.

My God, he thought. *I did not choose this love. It is beyond myself. I had thought that love developed and grew after marriage. That is what I was told. But this did not. It is so great I can scarcely believe it. It frightens me. I have hurt so many loved ones already. Let me not hurt this one. Let me be to her a guide and a blessing. Help her to abandon her false gods and look to me . . . and to You.*

Chapter Nine

Beeri came into the dining room, tying the brown cord of his long sand-colored robe. He observed Huldah's tight-lipped concentration as she fussed with the flower arrangement on the low wooden table. She had gone to greater lengths than usual to have the house spotless, the dinner perfect. She was dressed in one of her finest linen gowns and the color he liked: a sky blue interwoven with gold threads. Her graying hair was held back with mother-of-pearl combs.

"You're nervous, Huldah," he said, walking over to her.

She started when he spoke. Now she shook her head in bewilderment. "What's happening to us, Beeri? Not long ago everything seemed so right and good. Now everything has fallen apart."

Beeri faced her. "Is it that bad, Huldah?"

She had always admired Beeri's strength, the feeling of protection he gave her, as if they could face anything. Hosea was much like him in that way. Her voice was almost a whisper as she raised her troubled eyes to meet his. "Oh, Beeri, I never thought I'd see the day when we would allow a pagan woman to come into our house."

"You could have told Hosea not to bring her."

Huldah took a deep breath. She recalled when Hosea had asked her. His struggles of the past months had ceased. They had been replaced by a peace and a calm. She could not help but wonder what new thing he would confront them with next. First he could not be a priest, and then he could not marry Marabah.

But she would never, in her wildest dreams, have expected what came from him. "May I bring a woman to dinner, Mother?" he had asked. "She does not believe in God the way we do. But I want to help her believe." That was all he had said. Her son at that moment had seemed a stranger.

Huldah sighed. "No, Beeri. I couldn't tell Hosea not to bring her. He's not a child that we can forbid to do certain things. We must stand behind him if he is right in trying to help this woman. If he is not right, then he will need us more than ever."

"Let's not be hasty to pass judgment, Huldah," Beeri warned. "You know Hosea is not one just to talk about right and wrong, but to act upon it."

Huldah's eyes were skeptical. "You think that's all there is to this, Beeri?"

A worried expression passed his face, but Beeri did not reply, for Hosea's voice sounded in the inner court. It was followed by feminine laughter.

"They're here," Beeri said quickly. "Let's go and greet them."

Beeri held onto Huldah's arm as they walked into the inner court. The young woman was seated on the stone wall surrounding the fountain. She touched a delicate flower, murmured something to Hosea, lifting her face toward him. Huldah knew instantly the answer to the question she had asked Beeri. There was no mistaking the way Hosea and the young woman looked at each other.

Huldah and Beeri were almost upon them when Gomer quickly stood and faced them.

"Mother, Father," Hosea said in a gentle, deep voice. "This is Gomer."

Both Huldah and Beeri were amazed. In their minds they had built up a picture of a pagan woman who represented a forbidden idolatry, an abomination to their God. But here stood a young girl whose beauty was astonishing. Her oval face displayed a delicately formed forehead and chin, a straight, small nose and high cheekbones. Her black hair hung loose to her shoulders. The pale lavender dress of exquisite silk graced the trim lines of her maturing body.

"She lives beyond the brown hills in Bethel." The word *Bethel* reminded Huldah that the village contained a temple of Baal.

Gomer held out her hand to them. Her bare upper arm was adorned with a delicate gold bracelet. Bejeweled rings were on her slim, graceful fingers.

Never had Huldah or Beeri seen such a lovely face. Unflawed features, yet with an expression all its own. A natural pink graced her cheeks. Her pale, sensitive mouth greeted them with a smile of genuine warmth.

There was an awkward silence. "I believe we can go in to dinner now," Huldah said.

The four of them sat on couches around the low table. The succulent young kid was cooked to perfection. Fruits of their labors adorned the table. The best dishes were used. Wine was poured into their finest goblets. The young village girls who served were unable to hide their wide-eyed surprise and delight over the beautiful girl. Never had they seen one quite like her.

When Huldah had told them Hosea was bringing home an important guest, they had assumed it was the High Priest from the temple in Jerusalem and would have something to do with his priestly vows. This guest and the light conversation were a delightful contrast.

Gomer was excited over the breads and cakes that Huldah herself had made. "Hosea says you're an expert baker."

"I've been doing it for many years," she said, pleased with the compliment. "Do you cook, my dear?"

"Oh, no. I've never even tried. My time has been taken with singing and dancing and playing musical instruments. I teach children now." Gomer paused and looked toward Hosea, a look of uncertainty in her eyes. "My father, Diblaim, is a goldsmith. He taught me to make some things in gold."

"I know your father's reputation," Beeri said. "He is considered an expert. I understand his products are exported to other countries."

"Yes," Gomer admitted proudly. "His musical instruments are in particular demand. He also made this bracelet." She touched the bracelet on her arm.

"And the lyre she plays when teaching the children," Hosea added.

"That reminds me of King David," Huldah said dreamily. "I love the sound of the lyre." Then she added hastily, "You have such a musical voice, Gomer. I'm sure you must sing well."

"I don't know how well," Gomer replied, a faint blush on her cheeks. "But the children like it. We begin our lessons like this." She began to softly sing the words.

Raise your eyes to the god
Who makes a flower
Open your heart to the god
Who makes a tree
Lift your hands to the god
Who sends the sunshine
Sing to the god of all nature
For he made you and me.

Hosea smiled at Gomer with pride and deep affection. Then she raised her eyes toward the roof, placed her hands on her heart, lifted her arms in the air as she demonstrated how the children would sing.

"You teach me to play the lyre," Huldah teased, "and I will teach you one of my secret recipes."

Gomer laughed delightedly. "We will do it!" Her eyes were bright. "Wouldn't my family be surprised if I cooked something like this?" She took another bite of the delicious pastry.

Huldah observed that the servant girls took turns standing at the dining room archway and whispering among themselves. The night's events would be spread throughout Ephraim before morning. Poor Marabah! Those prayers about her would not be answered. She was quite sure now that any thought of Marabah no longer existed for Hosea. It was easy to see how her level-headed son could completely lose his head and heart to this girl.

In fact, she marveled that Hosea would have struggled for so long before making his decision concerning Gomer. This beautiful, sensitive girl couldn't possibly have any part of the gory rumors she had heard about pagan worship. She simply couldn't.

After dinner they walked from the dining room to the roof. Lamps of olive oil placed in the wall niches gave a soft glow to the inner court and along the steps leading past the second floor and onto the roof. A higher wall surrounded the area where couches, stools and tables sat. Huldah sat next to Beeri on a couch. Hosea and Gomer sat in chairs next to each other.

Moonlight glinted on the roof of a nearby building. "The building across the way is my bakery," Huldah said. "I'll have to show it to you when it's light."

Gomer expressed surprise. "I didn't think Hebrew women had careers. I suppose I have much to learn."

Huldah smiled. "I'm sure we all do. Sometimes we have

ideas in our minds without really knowing. That is not the way God would have us think."

Gomer leaned forward. She would not pretend any longer. They were surprised at the seriousness in her voice when she asked, "Where is your God?"

Chapter Ten

Huldah and Beeri were momentarily taken aback. Hosea was not. Already she had asked him the same question and he felt his answers had not satisfied her. "Is your God in the Temple at Jerusalem?" she pursued.

Beeri and Huldah had been as careful as she to avoid the subject. But now they seemed glad she had approached it. Huldah began to tell her the story of creation, man succumbing to sin, God's judgment.

Beeri related the story of God's guidance through the patriarchs, Abraham, Isaac, Jacob and Joseph; then the Egyptian slavery and Moses leading them through the wilderness and receiving the Ten Commandments.

Gomer listened with delight as they briefly scanned their history for her, telling of their judges and kings and leading up to the present time. She asked many questions about Rachel, Ruth and Deborah.

Finally Huldah laughed. "We cannot tell it all in one evening. We will talk again." Gomer was impressed. Jehovah was a magnificent God, she thought. It would be a wonderful thing if their God were represented at the temple of Baal.

"Do you have a statue of Him?" she asked.

"He is the Creator and sustainer of life," Beeri replied. "He is everywhere and dwells with all who allow Him. But," Beeri hastened to explain, "He forbids any image to be made of Him. We do not worship an object."

"He's invisible?" she asked.

"Yes," Beeri replied. "But He has manifested Himself to us in tangible ways."

Gomer was disappointed. She looked down quickly at her fingers entwined on her lap. She wondered how they could have a Temple and a belief with no representation. But they were so sincere.

"My father used to worship your God," she said, looking at them again. "But I don't believe he even thinks about it any more."

She looked down again after observing their quick glances at Hosea. He was not looking at them but had a set, hardened look about his face as he gazed out beyond them into the night. He had warned her it might be difficult. Then, it hadn't seemed to matter, for there had just been the two of them together. Nothing else had mattered but that.

But she could feel the tension now. Perhaps they thought she wanted to take him away from their God. She did not. She wanted to understand their God and have them understand hers. Maybe she should talk freely about her own. So she began to relate the names of her various gods and their purposes. Huldah and Beeri were expressionless. They did not meet her eyes, nor each other's.

"My mother has just retired as High Priestess of the temple," she continued. She told of her sister who had become High Priestess. She was neither embarrassed nor apologetic about what she believed and practiced. "I am a temple assistant. We do not worship the objects," she explained. "They are but symbols. And an aid to the beauty of the worship."

Gomer suddenly stopped talking. It seemed as if everything had stopped living except her own heart. Why did they not respond? Why did they look so stricken, as if some terrible thing had happened? Why did they no longer meet her eyes? It must be as Jothan said—that there are some foolish, ignorant people who refuse to face the truth. But Hosea was not foolish and ignorant. His parents did not seem to be, and she so wanted their acceptance. She felt a chill, and stood up suddenly.

Quickly Hosea was standing beside her. He grasped her hand in his, his face set in a fiercely determined way. His voice was low and deep. "We are going to marry."

Huldah and Beeri tried to speak but no words came out. The silence seemed interminable.

Huldah finally cleared her throat. "I—I've always wanted a—a daughter," she stammered. Then she walked over and gently laid her hands on Gomer's shoulders, leaned forward and kissed both cheeks.

"Welcome," she said, "to the family." Her trembling lips did not complete the intended smile.

"Thank you," Gomer replied breathlessly. She had not expected it to be so difficult. And she knew she was not the daughter Huldah wanted. Everything had gone so well until she talked about her gods. But she could not deny them. It would be against all that was sacred not to express how she felt.

Beeri reached out and touched Hosea's shoulder. "We will say goodnight, son," he said quietly. He then took Huldah's arm as they left the roof.

Hosea went over to Gomer, and embraced her.

"I thought they were going to turn you out," she said.

"For a moment, so did I," he replied.

"They don't like me." Tears were in her eyes.

"You're wrong. They like you very much. It's just hard for them to accept. It takes a while."

"Suppose no one will marry us? What will we do?" He had told her he would not be married by one of her priests, nor would any true priest or rabbi of Jehovah perform such a ceremony.

"If I must, I will take my vows, become a priest, and perform the ceremony myself," he replied adamantly.

Gomer's smile was tremulous. "I should have known you would find a way."

He looked at her lovely, upturned face, the soft, parted lips murmuring words of love, the violet eyes shining with excitement.

"Yes," he said and drew her head against his chest.

Above them a cloud, like a shadow, began to move across the moon. He admonished himself suddenly that there was no past, only a present and a future. Then he lifted her face with his fingertips, bent to gently, lingeringly kiss her lips until the shadow passed and the moon again shone brightly, without a cloud to obscure it.

Smiling down at her he said, "I'll take you home now."

Chapter Eleven

It was from Marabah's father that Jason heard the startling news about Hosea. Asa came to the Temple weekly to bring his tithe and almost always stopped by to talk with the priests. On this hot, dry day Asa's limp was more pronounced as he swiftly made his way toward Jason.

"I suppose you've heard about your friend Hosea?" he snapped.

His tone of voice and expression *your friend* surprised Jason. Asa was known to be an outspoken yet well-mannered man. He had always spoken fondly of Hosea as "my future son-in-law."

"I haven't seen Hosea in weeks," Jason replied. "What has happened?"

"What has not happened?" Asa replied, lifting his eyes toward the sky as they walked away from the Temple where their conversation would be more private. "First he said he was not going to become a priest, then he broke his engagement to Marabah."

Jason was only mildly surprised that Hosea did not intend to become a priest. Even though all he needed to do was take his vows, Hosea had confided to him his doubts. As for the broken engagement—well, the course of love was always uncertain. However, he was bewildered by Asa's next heated declaration.

"Now we learn that he is involved with a pagan woman, a goddess, they call her, from the temple of Baal."

At the startled look Jason gave him, Asa nodded. "Yes," he continued. "I couldn't believe it myself. But he took her to Huldah's and Beeri's for dinner. Their servants spread the word of this beautiful woman, dressed like a queen, who sang at their table. They all laughed and had a wonderful time."

"Unbelievable," Jason exclaimed.

"That's not all," Asa continued. "Their betrothal has been announced."

Jason was astounded. "You're sure these aren't just rumors?"

"I wish they were," Asa said. "Deborah and I went to Huldah and Beeri. They have confirmed it. They cried with us, apologized, but—" he shrugged. "Their son is a man. What can they do?"

"They could denounce him."

Asa shook his head. "Beeri and I talked about that. I suggested it might bring Hosea to his senses, but Beeri won't do that. They intend to stand by him."

Jason didn't know what to say. Hosea had never mentioned a pagan woman to him. But he was beginning to understand the reason for Hosea's troubled mind of the past months.

"It is a blatant rejection of all that is holy," Asa said loudly, uncaring that passersby could hear. "Another priest of God has fallen to the lure of pagan idolatry. Of course, I'm upset about my daughter and her broken heart. But more than that, Jason," he said fearfully, lowering his voice, "if one with Hosea's dedication and past abhorrence of idolatry can be turned, what hope is there? Many are going to be hurt by this. If Hosea has turned, then who will not?"

Shaking his head in anger, Asa grasped Jason's arm in a parting gesture and walked determinedly away.

Jason pondered Asa's words as he strode through the city streets, past a grove of olive trees, up a sloping path, and beyond the myriad of look-alike dwellings dotting the hillsides. His home was at the highest part of the hill, badly in need of repair and a fresh coat of white lime.

Stepping into the tiny courtyard surrounded by a clay brick wall, Jason felt his usual loneliness and reluctance to enter the house. The same broken bench was shoved against one side of the courtyard; broken pots littered the earthen floor; flower beds that used to be at full bloom this time of year were shrunken crusts of hard earth. Since Sarah died, he hadn't the heart to do much of anything to the house.

His shoulders sagged as he pulled over a couch to the side of the courtyard shaded by olive, fruit and pine trees. His unkempt hair fell over his forehead unnoticed. Lying back and closing his eyes, Jason tried to relax.

He was glad he had both his priestly and rabbinical duties. They filled his life with something meaningful. He was glad to return to the house that he and his wife had shared, but it was sad, too, for she was no longer here. He remembered when he had first brought her here. The walls had gleamed white in the sunlight then, and they had both been estatic with the pleasure of having their own home. He knew now how small it was, with only a receiving room and kitchen on the first floor, the two rooms above, and the flat roof. There was not even a courtyard at the back of the house, for it was set into the hillside. When Sarah was alive it had seemed like a mansion, and the view from the roof, from where they could even see the Temple, was as if God's special blessing had rested upon them.

Jason sighed, forcing his thoughts back to Hosea. He remembered the first time they met. Hosea had been brought to the Temple by Beeri. The boy had been taught everything Beeri could teach him and the bright-eyed youngster was eager to learn and ambitious to become a priest. Jason had thought that was typical of young devout Hebrews, but soon learned the seriousness of Hosea's intent. By the time Hosea was twenty years old, he was discussing not only the Scriptures but politics, economy and the ills of society with both priests and rabbis. After a while there no longer seemed to be a ten-year age span between them. They were just two men learning together and concerned about the world situation and the deterioration that had become so prevalent in Israel's social and religious life. It was accepted that God had given Hosea not only an uncanny insight into interpreting the Word of God, but also of prophecy.

It was Hosea who came to his home when Sarah lay dying of that dread wasting disease. She had died painfully and Hosea grieved with Jason. When the bereaved husband was especially distraught, Hosea came and walked and talked with him.

Jason realized suddenly that he was hungry and thirsty. If Sarah had been there she would already have brought him fruit or cheese. He smiled, thinking of her. It was good to have memories. Slowly he rose, wondering if there was anything to eat in the house. He laughed to himself, remembering that a friend had recently asked how he stayed so trim; that a man of thirty-five, graying at the temples, ought to at least have the courtesy to put on a few extra pounds around the middle. But, of course, that friend didn't realize he often forgot whether there was anything to eat in the house.

A woman from the city came in to clean occasionally, while two older men did a little work around the place. He hired them simply because they needed a job. When he remembered, he stocked up on supplies. Most of the time it slipped his mind.

He opened the wooden door that led into the storage room and found a jar of cool goat's milk plus some bread and cheese. As he sat eating at the table, he thought about his friend Hosea and how much he reminded him of the prophet Isaiah down in Judah, and Amos who used to speak out boldly in the Temple. Jason was well aware that men were capable of almost anything, that even devout priests of Jehovah had frequented the shrines of Baal. But Hosea? No, he could not believe Hosea had turned from God Jehovah.

Three days later, after a particularly trying day at the Temple, Jason trudged home for a little peace and quiet. He washed and changed. One of his part-time servants informed him that Hosea waited in the courtyard to see him.

After running a comb through his unruly hair, Jason hurried down the steps to greet Hosea. He noted that some of the worry had vanished from Hosea's eyes. But there was still fire there. No doubt he had been to the Temple where questions and accusations had been hurled at him.

"Welcome, Hosea." Jason grasped his friend's arm tightly. "I was just getting ready for supper. Join me."

Hosea hesitated. "I know you've heard things at the Temple, Jason. Maybe you would like to hear me out before you invite me to sit at your table."

Jason spoke quickly. "You're my friend, Hosea. You're always welcome in my house." Then he laughed. "But you look like you've rolled in the dirt."

"I've come a long way today," Hosea replied. "And I didn't bring a change of clothes."

'Go upstairs and wash. There are plenty of clothes. I can't guarantee that they're washed, though."

Hosea laughed and disappeared up the steps. He returned to find the table set with milk, cheese, bread and fruit.

"Sorry I don't have anything cooked to offer you," Jason apologized.

"This is plenty," Hosea assured him with a laugh. He broke off a piece of bread. "You're always apologizing, Jason, and it's quite unnecessary."

Jason shrugged. "I don't notice my scarcity until I have guests." He poured milk into cups.

Jason was determined not to press Hosea. He knew his friend would talk when he was ready. They ate silently until Hosea spoke. "You've heard statements about me, I'm sure."

"I've heard plenty," Jason replied.

"Do you believe the rumors?"

"I try not to believe rumors, Hosea," Jason replied, stroking his unkempt beard. Then he added seriously, "But even if you told me you had turned from God Jehovah, I would not believe it."

"I'm grateful for that." Hosea drained his cup and poured more milk.

"I've heard that you do not intend to take your priestly vows," Jason ventured.

"Are you surprised?"

"Not since I've given it some thought," Jason admitted. "You're trained and qualified to be either a priest or a rabbi or both. But I know the labels do not matter to you."

"Sometimes I think you're the only one who understands me, Jason," Hosea said with affection. He leaned forward, his forearms resting on the table. "But I may have to take my vows."

"Have to?" Jason queried.

"It's a difficult situation, Jason," he began seriously. "I am going to marry a woman who is a Baal worshiper."

The determined light in Hosea's eyes had replaced the troubled look of the past months. Jason responded with slightly raised eyebrows. Then he lowered his eyes to his cup of milk.

"As you well know," Hosea continued after a pause, "our religious code forbids me to marry her. I will not be married by a pagan priest nor one who combines Jehovah worship with Baalism. And gathering from the reception I received at the Temple today, none of the true priests of God will do it. So I may have to take my vows in order to perform my own marriage ceremony, unlawful or not."

"That's determination," Jason replied.

Hosea smiled as he met Jason's warm brown eyes. "I love her, Jason. I really love her. I have to save her from those deplorable practices." He looked down at his clasped hands on the table.

Jason stood. "Let's go up on the roof, Hosea. It will be cooler there now that the sun is setting."

There on the roof Jason reclined on a couch. Hosea walked over to the wall and looked out over olive groves, fig trees, date palms and flowering shrubs. From the roof he could see the city of Jerusalem. Soon the soft lights would glow from windows all over the hills and valleys.

"I've always liked your view here, Jason. It has a way of clearing my mind and putting things into perspective. I feel more objective up here, away from the crowds."

Hosea moved over to the couch and propped himself up in a sitting position with cushions behind his head. The extreme heat of the day was being pushed aside by a gentle cool breeze. The tranquil blue sky was slowly turning gray.

"Why don't you ask me to perform the marriage ceremony, Hosea?" Jason said finally.

Hosea shook his head. "I would not impose on your friendship, Jason. You are forbidden to do it and I would not allow it."

"Yet you will break the Law?" Jason asked.

"I would not break the Law readily," Hosea replied. "There are times when God's commands exceed the Law. He commands us not to kill, and yet at other times has commanded Israel to take up arms."

"And you feel God has commanded you to marry this woman?"

"I do," Hosea replied. "I can only hope it is not my own desires overruling the will of God."

Jason was convinced that Hosea would still be uncertain and struggling if he did not feel himself within the will of God. "I will perform the marriage ceremony for you."

Hosea sat up straighter and shook his head. "I can't ask you to do that, Jason."

"I know," Jason replied. "That's why I told you."

"You know it's forbidden."

"As you said, Hosea, God has the right to transcend His Law. If you believe this is right and part of God's will, then I concur with that."

"You need to know that this woman is an assistant High Priestess," added Hosea.

Jason shrugged off this information. "We will need to talk about the type of ceremony."

Both men were quiet for awhile, aware that there was no legitimate ceremony for a Hebrew and a Baal worshiper. She could not be legally considered a divorcee or a widow. The waiting period between the time of engagement and marriage, for a virgin, was a year.

"I met her about a year ago," Hosea said finally. "We will consider that we were engaged at that time. The wedding will take place in . . . two weeks."

"Two weeks?" Jason thundered.

"Well, Jason," Hosea stammered, the color rising on his face, "it's customary that the wedding take place three weeks after the betrothal is announced."

Jason did not bother to remind him that normally the plans are made during the year prior to the betrothal. But many plans were already made. The house was ready. Hosea and Marabah had done that.

"How is Marabah, Hosea?" Jason asked quietly.

"Marabah?" he replied absently. "She will be fine, Jason. I'm sure before long—perhaps already—she will realize what a mistake it would have been for us to marry."

"I never thought you cared about her the way she deserved to be cared about, Hosea."

"You're right," Hosea agreed. "She's a wonderful woman and will make someone an excellent wife. I care about Marabah much as I would a sister." He paused before continuing. "We never really loved each other, Jason."

"That is usually expected to come after marriage," Jason replied.

"I know. I suppose it would have. But I love Gomer without trying, without wanting to. It's just there and I can't escape it."

"I understand, Hosea," Jason said, thinking of his wife, whom he had loved almost from the first time he met her.

Jason stood and put his hand on Hosea's shoulder, feeling a sudden and deep concern for Marabah, a lovely and proud woman.

"God forgive us," Jason said, almost a prayer, "if we're not right in this."

Chapter Twelve

The day before the wedding, Jason stood on the roof of Huldah's and Beeri's house looking out over the front courtyard and the early morning dew that covered the fields beyond. As officiating rabbi and intermediary between Hosea and Gomer, he had been extremely busy during the past two weeks. He was the one who bore Hosea's gifts to Gomer and her family. They had been greatly pleased with the abundance of fine materials and jewels. Gomer had been delighted with the mother-of-pearl chest inlaid with gold, the silver polished mirror with her name engraved on the handle and the jewelry she would wear on her wedding day.

"You must let me know what you think of my present to Hosea," she had said, her voice breathless.

"I think it's perfect," Jason had replied immediately.

"You don't think he will mind that my family is a part of it? I mean, I know how Hebrews feel."

Jason's warm brown eyes had clouded momentarily. Hosea had insisted there be nothing in the ceremony to indicate Baalism, and of course he himself would have no part in such things. Looking at Gomer made him think of things like springtime, morning dew, first ray of dawn, sweet notes of music, a gentle rain.

His troubled eyes had looked away from hers when she

asked his approval of the gift she had prepared. It was no child's mind that had conceived this bit of artistry. There was brilliance, creativity, maturity of thought that might surpass even that of the Temple artisans in Jerusalem. And Jason knew that behind and beyond her perfect beauty and her natural warmth toward people lay an unusual subtlety. Hosea must surely know that his bride-to-be was of extraordinary wisdom and intelligence and would challenge his own. Of course he knew. He would not marry a woman who was less.

"I am certain he will know how to appreciate such a gift," Jason had said at last, warmed by her pleased expression.

Now, as he stood on the roof in the early dawn, he felt her smile had been much like the sky, its first rays of sun bringing a natural warmth with a gentle pink glow, chasing away the gray of the night.

He turned suddenly. There was much to be done. He had to see Hosea at his house to finalize plans. He would need to rehearse with Gomer and her wedding party. The entire second floor of Huldah's and Beeri's house was ready for Gomer and her attendants who would arrive early tomorrow morning.

Already the baking that would go on for the entire day had begun. Soon, village women with their profusion of flowers would be decorating the house and courtyards. Barrels of wine must be set out in every corner. Tables for the wedding feast must be set up on the back court. He must remember to have the crowns ready. And there was the canopy to erect on the front courtyard. Stools, tables, chairs, pots, everything must be moved to leave as much space as possible for dancing. This was a wedding that no one would want to miss—except for Marabah and her parents.

Jason thought of that several times during the day as he had during the past weeks. One evening he had walked away from the activity of the house and through the grove of fig trees toward the dusty streets of the village. He was almost upon the dark-hooded figure before she turned suddenly and gave a startled gasp.

"Jason," she said. "What are you doing here?"

"I thought I would talk to your father, Marabah."

"At the moment he is talking with two priests, who at my father's suggestion are considering naming Hosea's wedding a farce—illegal and against the teaching of God." Her tone held bitterness. "It may not be accepted by the council, Jason. Why don't you join them and convince them that it's all right for a follower of Jehovah to marry an idolater? Surely you can persuade them of that, Jason, since you are convinced of it yourself." She turned away sharply and the hood fell from her head.

"Marabah," he said softly and she stopped, her back toward him. "I only wanted you and your family to know that I understand that you are hurt. And I care about you all. But if your father has guests, I will not intrude. Perhaps it's best that I found you here alone."

"Alone?" she said suddenly, and whirled around, facing him. "What else could I be, Jason? My fiance is getting married tomorrow. I can't walk out of the house during the daylight without someone telling me how sorry they are, or talking about evil spirits luring Hosea away, or asking me about it, or giving me sympathetic looks. But I suppose I will just have to get used to hiding away at night, being alone." With that she turned and walked quickly away.

Jason strode beside her and caught hold of her arm, but she jerked away.

"Are you angry with me, Marabah?" he asked.

She stopped then and with a bitter laugh looked toward the bright moonlit sky. "Why should I be angry? Hosea always said the nation of Israel was turning to idolatry. Now he has proved it. And you"—her eyes flashed accusingly—"you, a priest and rabbi, would break the laws and perform the ceremony. Yes, I am angry. And hurt. And confused."

She looked so helpless that his heart went out to her.

"Marabah," he said softly. "Do you honestly believe Hosea and I have turned from God?"

A long sigh escaped her throat. "I don't know, Jason. I don't know what to think right now."

"If Hosea's heart is not in tune with the true God—if he could be swayed toward idolatry—aren't you fortunate to know now?"

"It's hard to accept, Jason. All I can see right now is that if it's God's will, then God is punishing a Hebrew woman and favoring a pagan idolater. Why does the Lord want me to face a future alone? Why must I be bitter toward that woman—and God?"

"It's only human that you should feel so, Marabah," Jason consoled quietly. "I felt I needed my wife so much, and yet she is gone. Some things are of the world, some are of God, some are of evil. I cannot always discern."

Marabah felt suddenly ashamed. "I'm sorry if I spoke abruptly, Jason," she said, drawing in her breath. "I know the facts of life. And I will face them. I will be glad later on, perhaps. But you must forgive me if I can't do that just yet."

"Why don't you take off that cloak, Marabah? It must be quite warm."

She obeyed. Jason took it from her and folded it over one arm as they began walking back in the direction from which they had come.

"You do . . . love him, Marabah?"

He took her arm when they came to the trees and stepped into the shadows, then placed her cloak on a low branch and leaned back against a tree. Marabah stood near him. After a while she answered.

"I didn't know that was a requirement for marriage, Jason."

"Normally it isn't. With most of us marriage happens because we are first attracted to each other, then begin liking each other enough to let parents know so they can make proper arrangements. Love is usually something that grows as the years go by. But sometimes, Marabah, it comes first—unexpectedly."

She nodded. "Yes. What you are talking about is something called love, but is it that? That's what it's called when a man or woman leaves a spouse for another person. When engagements are broken. And . . . when a good man leaves the true God for a pagan woman. Is that love?" She paused for a deep breath. "All right. Suppose that's love. Perhaps it's wonderful for the person who experiences it. But what about the one left behind? What about me?"

"Why don't you tell me about it, Marabah?" he asked quietly.

She leaned back against the tree, facing Jason but looking beyond him. Gradually her face relaxed and a softness came into her features as she related the facts concerning her lifelong friend to whom she had been promised so many years ago.

"I never questioned it, Jason," Marabah continued. "Even when Hosea kept postponing the wedding, I never dreamed we would not marry. But of course," she said, resentment again creeping into her tone, "I never thought a pagan woman could turn Hosea's head."

"Neither did he, Marabah," Jason replied. "It is the pagan part that would turn him away, not lure him. Surely you know that." He paused, then added quietly, "They love each other, Marabah."

Marabah drew in her breath and turned her head away. "I've never seen a pagan woman, Jason," she said, her voice unsteady. "What does she look like?"

Jason didn't answer immediately. He looked beyond her, then felt her eyes on him. "An angel," he said finally.

Marabah gasped and looked in the direction he was looking, wondering if he were seeing a vision. "An angel?"

"Any other words would be inadequate."

Marabah felt uncomfortable. "I've never seen . . . an angel."

"Neither have I, Marabah. I didn't say she is one. I said she looks like one."

"Your description does not fit the person I had in mind."

He smiled tenderly at her. "I know. We have been taught how vile and evil and obscene the worship of Baal is. And it is, in its truest sense. But do you think so many of our priests would have turned from Jehovah to Baal if this god had appeared obscene, undesirable, vile, evil?"

"Hosea is among the strongest followers of Jehovah," Marabah said slowly.

"Exactly," Jason agreed. "It is the strong who are the targets of the evil one."

Marabah stared. "What are you saying, Jason?"

"I'm saying, Marabah, that our beloved Hosea, a man of God, is already influential among the rabbis and priests. His eloquent words have already brought responses from the king himself. Who do the people of the village go to when they want a religious question answered? Who do they look to in matters they are unable to deal with? Whose wisdom and insight do they seek?"

Comprehension began to settle in Marabah's large brown eyes.

"You see, Marabah, Hosea is a leader. He is a strong one.

There are many priests of Jehovah right now who are delighted that Hosea is marrying Gomer because it eases their conscience about going to the shrines of Baal. There are those in this village who are toying with the idea of combining their worship with that of Baal. Hosea's marriage will reinforce that. The most promising young man in all of Israel is marrying a worshiper of Baal. It's not just a man and woman in love, Marabah. This is much, much more. It is a battle between God and Baalism. It is not a time for abandoning Hosea, but standing by him, believing in him and his faith in God."

Marabah was thoughtful before speaking. "I suppose I can understand that. But this is personal to me, Jason. Surely you can't expect me to act as if nothing has happened."

"No one expects that of you, Marabah," he replied. "Tomorrow during the wedding, everyone will sympathize with you, sitting alone in your room crying brokenheartedly."

"Really, Jason," Marabah said in exasperation.

"Isn't that what you're going to do?"

"What do you expect me to do? Go to the wedding?"

"I would expect a sensible girl like you, Marabah, to convince your parents that they should not let a lifetime friendship be destroyed by this. I would hope that you would admit to them that this is not a matter of the heart so much as a matter of pride."

"Whatever it is, Jason," she replied angrily, "you can't expect me to change overnight. I've thought one way for twenty-four years. It's—difficult."

"Of course it's difficult. But you talk about not wanting to face the future alone. When do you intend to start doing something about it?"

"It takes time," she said weakly.

"Yes," he agreed. "But one who waits too long can become bitter and cynical."

Sighing, she looked at him. "Jason, I've become realistic during the past few months. I don't want to spend my life alone, but I also know that everyone my age has been married for many years. Nobody seems to want an older woman." She lifted her shoulders helplessly. "There's no one but old men who. . . ." Her voice trailed off.

Jason knew what she was about to say and his heart was stirred. The moonlight shone soft on her face. Her wordless lips parted in surprise as she felt the warmth and affection he now allowed her to see in his expression.

Jason brought her cloak and lay it around her shoulders. Marabah looked toward the village street, then faced Jason with uncertain eyes. Tears sprang to the surface. "Oh, Jason," she wailed and he drew her to him.

"Cry," he said. "It's good for you."

Jason remembered that he had once promised Sarah he would never hold another woman in his arms. But just before she died Sarah had said that he should marry again. He hadn't thought he ever would. But Sarah was right—it was not good to be alone.

When Marabah's sobbing subsided, she looked up and studied his face with her frank brown eyes. He was moved by the way the tears had gently caressed her cheeks and the moonlight lay softly on her lips.

Standing at the edge of the trees, Jason watched in admiration as Marabah placed the dark cloak on her arm and walked slowly, proudly in the bright moonlight, down the village street.

Chapter Thirteen

The wedding festivities began at daybreak. Contests were held, games played. Then it was time for singing, dancing, drinking wine and eating. Village women attempted to outdo each other with the food they had brought.

Mainly because of Jason's words—that everyone would expect her to sit home in a corner crying—Marabah arose early and persuaded her parents that they should not take any public action against Hosea, but instead should go to his wedding. There was a spirited family debate before Marabah's viewpoint was accepted. When they arrived at the wedding, the festivities were in full swing.

Beeri appeared immediately, clasped Asa's hands vigorously. Deborah and Huldah embraced, cried a little, then Deborah asked to be put to work. Except for the restraint in Asa's eyes, the old relationship seemed restored.

Marabah's pasted-on smile was soon genuine. She graciously thanked her friends for their compliments on her new dress and didn't bother to tell them it was one she had chosen for her own wedding trip. The deep rust-colored silk was gracefully draped over her full figure, giving her a femininity she rarely exposed. A golden sheen embraced her auburn hair. She had even dared to brush her cheeks with artificial color.

Sampling the food and sipping from her wine goblet, Marabah had felt little apprehension until the shout sounded, "The bridegroom is coming!"

Then the color drained from her face, and she was grateful no one was looking at her. All were trying to get inside the inner court. "Let's go where we can see," a friend said, pulling her along.

She had meant to stay outside, perhaps at a doorway so she could leave if she wanted to, but found herself pushed into the inner court.

Hosea and Jason came in together. Hosea was smiling, radiant. He was handsome in his light blue robe with the deep blue trim, embroidered with white designs down the front and around the bottom. The troubled look of past months was gone.

Her eyes shifted to Jason. She was startled by the change in his appearance. His beard was neatly trimmed, his hair shortened. There was an aura of vitality about him that had been absent since Sarah's death. His long blue robe was appliqued with scarlet pomegranates around the bottom. Interspersed with the pomegranates were golden bells that tinkled when he walked. Over the ephod was an elaborately jeweled breastplate. She knew any woman would be proud to be with a man like Jason, but it was not easy to shift one's interest from one man to another, literally overnight.

The ten groomsmen lined up across the inner court at the staircase. Flutists played softly. Ten lovely young bridesmaids in light blue dresses, carrying bouquets of assorted flowers, ascended the staircase. The groomsmen offered their arms and they went into the outer court.

There were gasps, feet shuffling and murmuring when Rizpah appeared at the top of the steps, then slowly began to walk down them. She wore a white dress embroidered with tiny blue rosebuds. The skirt was split on each side to the knees. Regally, proud and smiling, she descended the stairs. Those who did not know might think Rizpah's beauty would surely overshadow the bride's.

When Gomer appeared at the head of the stairs, however, Rizpah was forgotten. There were no gasps, no murmurs, no shuffling, no voices—only the sound of the flutist. Gomer's beauty was breathtaking. The white silk gown, simply cut, fell in soft folds to the floor. The fingertip veil did not cover her face, but was fastened at the back of her head and covered the black hair that fell softly below her shoulders. She also wore a mother-of-pearl necklace, arm bracelets and an ankle bracelet that Hosea had given her.

Her radiant face and violet eyes met Hosea's. He held out his arm to her and they walked out onto the front court, followed by Jason and the crowds. The raised dais, covered in dark blue fabric, had been set up at the far end of the court. On it sat two highbacked chairs. Overhead was a blue-and-white canopy interwoven with golden threads and bordered with white fringe.

As soon as the crowd quieted, Hosea and Gomer knelt before Jason, who placed a small golden crown on Gomer's head and a larger jeweled one on Hosea's. They stood and Hosea turned to Gomer, placing a ring on her finger as he said, "Behold, you are consecrated unto me with this ring according to the Law of Moses and Israel."

A goblet of wine was handed to Jason, who passed it to Gomer to sip, and she in turn passed it to Hosea. Jason turned to the crowd, saying in a loud voice, "Let the festivities begin."

The king and queen were to be honored by their subjects on their wedding day. They sat in chairs. The crowd moved back against the walls as the entertainment began. Children from

Ephraim placed flowers on the dais, then sang love songs that King David and King Solomon had written.

Young lads who were students at the Temple in Jerusalem danced to the sound of flutes, timbrels, trumpets, cymbals and tambourines. Their energy seemed boundless and the crowd loved it.

After several displays of musical talent by villagers and Temple musicians, Jason stood again before the crowd. "The bride will now present her present to the groom."

Hosea looked at Gomer with surprise. This was unexpected. She smiled at him with a twinkle in her eyes and looked out toward the center of the court. A young man ran from the crowd onto the court and collapsed while a dramatic chord was struck on a harp. Rizpah, now dressed in a peasant girl's costume, rushed to the fallen figure. As a flute sounded a mournful medley, she wept. The dance of grief began, and the crowd was caught up in the story from the very beginning.

It began with spoken words of poetry, and dramatic dancing and artistry so effective that even the Temple artisans looked at each other in surprised approval. The story of Ruth then unfolded before their eyes. The dramatic scene of young Ruth leaving her own country and her own people brought tears to the eyes of onlookers. Her faith in God despite poverty was portrayed reverently and beautifully. Jothan, acting the part of Boaz, ceased to be a Baal High Priest for the moment and became a beloved Jewish historical character.

The ten bridesmaids and groomsmen danced and sang as they provided the mood of each scene, whether sorrow, grief, hunger, love or joy.

As Hosea watched the performance, he knew there were no greater professionals in the arts than these worshipers of Baal. Furthermore, as they acted out the characters and story that belonged to his own history and his own people, he was aware as never before that these people, despite their pagan ways, were creations of the true God, and that it was He who had given them such talents.

When it ended, the crowd applauded loudly, shouting words of praise to God and to their beloved King David, the grandson of Ruth. Then came words of good wishes to the bride and groom.

Jason finally silenced them with his hand. He held a leather-bound scroll. "The story of Ruth, as you have just seen, was compiled by the bride. She has written the poetry and the music and the dance for it. It has been approved and blessed by the High Priest of the Temple in Jerusalem and a copy will be placed there for our enjoyment, and as part of the masterpieces of literature and music that are collected and kept there. We are greatly honored to be in possession of such a work, as I am sure you all agree. Our thanks to the wonderful performance that has been enacted by the bride's family and friends."

"Marvelous!" Hosea said to Gomer as the impact of it had left him speechless for a moment. "It is a most wonderful gift, and I shall never forget it."

Jason presented a brief speech about marriage and quoted from the writings of King David. Then he turned to the bride and groom, asking them to stand. He read the marriage contract signed by two witnesses and gave it to Hosea. Hosea handed it to Gomer, saying, "Behold, you are consecrated unto me with this deed according to the Law of Moses and of Israel."

The wine was passed to them both and they sipped from the goblet. Then Hosea turned to Gomer, saying, "Become my wife according to the Laws of Moses and Israel, and I will work for you, honor you, provide you food, and take care of you, according to the existing statutes for Israelite husbands, who in good faith work for their wives, honor them, take care of them, and clothe them."

Jason then pronounced the seven benedictions. The couple removed their crowns and knelt before him. Holding his hand over their heads, he repeated the final benediction.

"Blessed art Thou, who has created joy and gladness, bridegroom and bride, mirth and exultation, pleasure and delight, love, brotherhood, peace and friendship. Soon, O Lord our God, may there be heard in the cities of Judah and in the streets of Jerusalem the voice of joy and gladness, the voice of the bridegroom and the bride, the jubilant voice of bridegrooms from their marriage chambers and of youths from their feasts of song. Blessed art Thou, O Lord, who makes the bridegroom to rejoice with the bride."

They stood. Jason stepped down and a glass was handed to him. He placed it on the stone beneath the dais. There was breathless silence as Hosea stepped down, raised his foot, then brought it forcefully down on the glass, splintering it into a hundred pieces. The silence was then broken by shouts of joy and music. Hosea held out his hand to Gomer. "You are my wife!" he said.

Giving him her hand, she asked, "Now what?"

Lifting his eyebrows he replied, "We dance!" They laughed together as they whirled about the courtyard while all the spectators applauded and shouted for them.

"Join in!" Jason shouted to the crowd. The bridesmaids and groomsmen began to dance, then Athalia and Diblaim, Rizpah and Jothan.

Beeri touched Huldah's arm. She looked at him. He moved his eyes toward the dance floor. She appeared shocked, then shrugged and they laughed as they danced. Asa and Deborah followed. By this time Jason had made his way to Marabah and held out his hand.

"Why, Jason," she said, pretending to be appalled. "You know Israelite men and women don't dance together." But she took his hand as they began to step in time with the music.

"People do things at weddings they do no other time," Jason replied.

Sitting next to Jason at the banquet table, Hosea watched proudly as learned men of the Temple—priests, rabbis and artisans—stopped to speak to Gomer. In their faces was the recognition that his wife was not just a beautiful woman, but one of exceptional intelligence and ability.

He smiled at the ease with which Gomer greeted people, asking about them personally, where they lived, what they did, about their children, thanking them for making her wedding day so lovely.

Jason leaned toward him. "This day will be remembered for a long time, Hosea. Your wife surprised everyone. What did you think of her gift to you?"

"Exceptional in its construction and execution."

"It was very obliging of her family to give such a performance," Jason commented.

Hosea turned the wine goblet in his fingers. "Was it?" he asked, a wry smile touching his lips. "Or did they see this as a great opportunity to show the good side of Baalism?"

Jason studied his friend's face. "Do you think that was Gomer's intention?"

"Only indirectly. She loves me. She wanted to please me. Her intentions are right. Still—" Hosea paused and his eyes clouded. "One cannot embrace God Jehovah without first forsaking idolatry. She has not done that."

"Will you tell her these things?"

"How, Jason? How do you look into the eyes of one you love

and who loves you and say, 'Thank you, but you are wrong'? It cannot be said or done in so few words."

Jason's voice was quiet when he asked, "Do you think she will forsake her gods?"

"I have to believe that, Jason," he answered.

Hosea arose, stretched out his hand toward Gomer and smiled into her eyes. "We will go home now."

Her smile was tender and expectant as she rose from her chair. The newly married couple then quietly escaped from the festivities through a side door in the court.

Chapter Fourteen

Hosea stood at the small window of the nursery, watching the stormclouds gather in the east. The afternoon had been beautiful, with slanting rays of the setting sun reflecting the orange-golden hue of the sky, giving the stone structure a look of burnished gold. Now the sun had sunk behind the hills, the color had faded, and the cool breeze that touched his face held a hint of rain. His tall frame shivered as he closed the shutters.

He turned to look down at the sleeping child. How often he and Gomer stood and spoke of the miracle they had produced: their first child—a boy named Jezreel. The wonder of it never left her voice. Leaning over, he tucked the blanket closer around the sleeping form. The carpet cushioned his steps as he left the room.

Passing Gomer's bedroom, he saw that she still sat before her mirror, taking extra care with her face and hair for the guests who were coming. As he descended the wide sweeping staircase covered with scarlet carpet, his hand caressed the long curved banister that bore the mark of Diblaim's craftsmanship: a long, fine line of gold that ran the entire length of the polished cypress wood.

Hosea looked up at the great cedar beams supporting the roof of the two-story structure. No sunlight filtered through the skylights, for a dull grayness had settled over the openings. There must be no gloom for their guests, so he quickly summoned a servant to light the lamps that brought a brilliant glow to the gleaming white marble floor of the inner court, enhancing the pool in the center of the room that was surrounded by statues, shrubs and lovely flowers.

Lamps were lighted in the blue-carpeted receiving room. The brazier was ready to be fired, should the evening grow cooler. The elegantly carved couches were made of cypress from Lebanon, covered with light blue velvet and adorned with colorfully embroidered cushions and fringed shawls.

A sweet fragrance permeated the room as soon as Gomer entered through the archway. Hosea's loving eyes devoured the long, graceful lines of the violet-colored silk that hugged her perfect figure and vividly enhanced the color of her eyes.

"I believe you are even lovelier as a mother," Hosea said tenderly. "Have I told you that?"

"Only every day for the past three months," Gomer replied, laughing.

"You're looking forward to tonight," Hosea commented, drawing her to him. Gomer nodded and lay her head against the brown stripes of his silk robe.

Hosea had steadily refused to allow the slightest apprehension to mar the most wonderful year of his life. Controversial topics had been avoided. Meanwhile, Gomer had used her creative touches to turn his house into their home. The result was much more beautiful than the simplicity of furnishings he had once imagined. She and Huldah had spent much time together so that Gomer could learn to make delicate pastries that he liked. Servants did the basic cooking but she enjoyed planning the meals.

They had gone into Jerusalem where he had shown her the Temple. She thought it magnificent but spoke with regret that women could not frequent the Temple as men, and that they could not share priestly duties.

Hosea had spent most of his time supervising his father's farms. After work he would hurry home, where his beautiful wife would be waiting, the child growing inside her. "I'm losing my figure," she would say.

"No," he disagreed. "You're finding it," and they would laugh and embrace and sometimes dinner would grow cold waiting for them. The servants would whisper. It did not matter. Life was wonderful and they were in love. As the baby grew and they felt increasingly proud of the miracle they had wrought, they would lie awake late at night with Hosea's hand on her stomach, feeling the movement of their child.

"Our happiness will never end, will it, Hosea?" she would ask sometimes.

"No," he would answer. "It will not end."

And tonight he must not show any display of jealousy or apprehension. He had thought it no longer a part of him, but as the time grew nearer for Gomer's family to visit he knew, deep inside, it was there.

"It's been a long time since you've seen your sister," he commented casually. He did not add, "And Jothan."

"I feel a little strange about Rizpah coming here to visit," Gomer confessed. "If I . . . if I lost my child"—Hosea noticed she did not say *sacrificed*—"it would be hard for me to see someone else happy with hers."

Hosea knew that Gomer missed her family. After Athalia's retirement, she and Diblaim had made a trip to Tyre, then into Phoenicia, visiting temples and priests they had known throughout the years. After their return, they visited several times with Hosea and Gomer. Jothan and Rizpah had not. Rizpah sent word that she was happy for them, but was too busy with temple activities and her new duties as High

Priestess to come. Gomer had gone once to the palace to tell Rizpah about her pregnancy. Jothan had not been at home.

A young servant girl came into the room, announcing that the guests had arrived. Diblaim and Athalia, the first to enter, kissed Gomer and greeted Hosea warmly. They now appeared comfortable in the home of a Hebrew. Hosea wondered if Diblaim had any poignant memories of his Jewish boyhood.

"We're grandparents," Athalia exclaimed. "And we're getting old, Diblaim."

"You'll never be old, my dear," he replied.

"That's the kind of remark I was seeking," she laughed.

Hosea shook hands cordially with Jothan, then turned to watch Rizpah and Gomer embrace.

"I'm sorry it's been so long," Rizpah apologized. "Now let me look at you." Gomer turned around in a light, dancing step, displaying her supple figure that showed no after-effects from the pregnancy.

"You are as trim as ever," Rizpah complimented her.

"And you look radiant," Gomer responded. "No signs of your illness."

Rizpah smiled, but Hosea detected what seemed to be an undercurrent of tension in Rizpah.

"I believe the guest of honor is here," Hosea said, glancing toward the archway where a servant had appeared with a small, bundled-up object howling loudly.

Gomer held out her arms for the baby. She cooed and stroked him. He settled down almost immediately once he was in his mother's arms. Sticking two fingers into his mouth, he began to suck on them.

"He's demanding his dinner," she said. Suddenly aware that she had not given Jothan a proper welcome, Gomer offered the baby to her guest. "Would you like to hold him?"

Startled, Jothan backed away.

Was not a priest of Baal accustomed to holding infants? Hosea wondered.

"Why are men so afraid of little babies?" Athalia asked in exasperation, casting a sly glance toward Jothan. "Give him to me." But Rizpah quickly moved forward and took the baby from Gomer's arms.

Tears began to form in her eyes. "He's so small," she whispered, and began to rock the infant back and forth very gently. An uncomfortable silence was broken by the return of the servant woman for the baby. "His dinner must not be delayed," Gomer explained.

When Hosea began talking to Athalia and Diblaim about the gardens they had started, Gomer took Rizpah and Jothan on a tour of the house.

"It's too cool to go on the roof," Gomer said as they walked across the inner court past the pool. "So we'll start with the second floor and work our way back down. Dinner will be ready by then."

"Such a gorgeous house," Rizpah remarked as they ascended the stairs. "Everything has worked out so well for you, Gomer. You and Hosea make a perfect couple. Few men are so good-looking, you know." Then Rizpah flashed a teasing glance toward Jothan. "Except for my husband." And she slipped her arm through his.

But Jothan was looking at Gomer. "Will Hosea be joining you in the temple?"

A slight sadness crossed her face. "I think he would do anything in the world for me except that. I don't think there's any chance of it."

"With time, Gomer," Jothan encouraged, "don't you think he might at least bring his God to our worship? It's not as if we forbid Jehovah worship. Surely you can make him understand that."

Gomer spoke with both sadness and respect. "He doesn't make hurried decisions. He will listen to arguments, but once he makes up his mind he will not be persuaded differently. He is convinced Jehovah is the only true God."

They walked along the spacious hallway on the second floor. Gomer took a lamp from a wall niche and paused outside a room. "You may look in," she said after a pause. "But you shouldn't go inside. This is Hosea's study, where he worships God, studies and prays." She opened the door.

Silently they looked inside. Shutters covered a single small window. One straight chair stood behind a long wooden table in the center of the hardwood floor. Scrolls, parchment, inkwells and pens cluttered the table. Along one wall was a shelf onto which additional scrolls and pieces of parchment had been placed. In one corner was a rolled-up mat.

"Does he talk about his studies?" Rizpah asked.

"Sometimes. He knows a great deal about the Scriptures," Gomer answered.

Gomer closed the door and led them into Hosea's bedroom, another room of simple and practical furnishings, excepting the luxurious brown carpet. A huge cedar bed dominated the room. Its position beneath the skylight would allow one to view a starlit sky, a yellow moon in its fullness, lightning streaking the sky in a violent storm. Tonight there was only darkness.

Gomer's adjoining bedroom was in sharp contrast to her husband's. Careful matching colors had been selected—a lavender canopy over the bed; yellow silk covering the dressing table bench; dark blue carpet and silk curtains with golden tassles. This room with its elegance, luxury, was not that of a Hebrew woman.

Jothan went to the dressing table and picked up the statue of Ashtoreth he had given her. "Will you return to the temple, Gomer?" he asked.

"Of course," Gomer replied immediately.

"Hosea won't mind?" Rizpah questioned.

"I don't mind if he worships his God," Gomer replied. "He doesn't feel that way about ours, but he knows this is my life, my career. He knows I'm not a Hebrew woman."

Rizpah started to reply, then checked herself.

"Jothan," Gomer said, turning toward him, her voice low and secretive. "I would like for you to bless the baby. Would you do that?"

"I would be delighted to bless my nephew," he assured her.

"Hosea probably won't like it," she said sadly, "but I didn't object when he named the boy Jezreel and had him circumcised."

The servant had just finished feeding the child when they entered the nursery. She excused herself and left the room, and Jothan picked up the baby. The blessing was pronounced hurriedly, the infant laid back on his mat, and the threesome stealthily departed. When they returned to the first floor, it was time for dinner.

The large dining area was separated by several columns. The floor of one half was white marble and on it was a long, narrow table inlaid with mother-of-pearl. On the other side of the columns was a scarlet carpet. Gomer laughed delightedly. "Hosea had that done." She flashed an affectionate glance toward him. "That is my dancing room."

"What a thoughtful thing to do!" Rizpah directed her comment to Hosea, who smiled and nodded toward the servants to bring the towels, dampened in rose water, for his guests to wipe their hands. They seated themselves around the table, graced with flowers from the garden and lighted by candles. At various points in the room, alabaster lamps hung from the ceiling on silver chains.

The expected exclamations concerning the elaborate meal

were made and graciously accepted. Gomer's family was surprised to learn that she had made the pastries.

The conversation turned again to the infant. "Why did you name him Jezreel?" Rizpah asked curiously.

"The name Jezreel has many meanings," Hosea began. Then he explained that Jezreel was the fertile, flourishing valley that many believed to have been sown by God Himself, it was so beautiful and fruitful. He also described the city of Jezreel where King Jehu had shed much blood.

"The word Jezreel means *judgment is sure.* There will come a day when God's judgment will inflict punishment on the house of King Jehu," Hosea said sternly. "He took up the worship of golden calves. He did not walk according to the laws of God."

"I will think of Jezreel as a symbol of that lovely valley," said Rizpah firmly. "He is a precious child."

Hosea noticed that his words had made Diblaim acutely uncomfortable. *I must try to win him back to the true God,* he thought to himself.

Rizpah had been enjoying the evening immensely. She was delighted to see how happy Gomer was in her new home. Although she felt that Hosea's naming his child Jezreel was rather strange, she found herself liking the man who directed the conversation toward her. She could not help but wish that either he would become a part of their temple worship, or that he would keep Gomer away. She alone in her family did not think Gomer was an asset to their temple.

Rizpah also had a special announcement to make and she waited for the right moment. Finally it came. With joy in her eyes and pink in her cheeks, she asked for their attention. "I am with child," she said shyly. At that moment, she could almost compete with her younger sister's beauty.

With an unrestrained exclamation of delight, Gomer rose

from her chair and ran over to embrace Rizpah. The others followed. With great relief Rizpah noted that Jothan's pleasure over the news was as great, perhaps greater, than anyone else's.

Before leaving, Rizpah had one more conversation with Hosea. "While you are having a child, who will become Jothan's High Priestess?" he finally asked her.

"A temple assistant will take my place for a few months," she replied, watching his face carefully.

The slight nod of his head indicated it was a casual answer to a simple question. But noting the sudden tightening of his lips and darkening expression in his brown eyes, Rizpah felt a sudden kinship with her brother-in-law.

Chapter Fifteen

A gnawing uneasiness grew inside Hosea in the days following the dinner when Rizpah announced that she was pregnant. He told himself that Gomer would never return to the temple, not after their wonderful year together. He tried not to think about the golden statue she kept in her room. He tried to avoid the fact that she had not accepted God Jehovah any more than he had accepted her pagan idols. Their love was still there, but now with a slight blemish.

"I want to go to Mother's," she said several times. He looked quickly away from her eyes that seemed to dare him to protest.

One warm night they sat on the roof, a pleasant respite after several days of rain. Gomer was restless. Suddenly she was on her feet, facing Hosea. "I must go," she whispered and he knew what she meant.

"No," he replied, shaking his head.

"Please understand," she said, her eyes pleading.

"That you want to go to another man?"

"No," she gasped. "Don't say things like that. I don't want another man. But I must worship my gods. I belong there. Now that Rizpah can't be there, I am obligated."

Hosea had difficulty keeping his voice calm. "What about your obligation to me? To our marriage vows? Our child? Do these suddenly mean nothing?"

"How can you question it?"

"Then don't go."

"I'll be back."

"I forbid it," he said flatly.

"You can't forbid that," she said. "I am not your slave. You knew when you married me that your silly, confining laws cannot apply to me. You knew that."

"I thought my love for you meant something."

"It means everything. But I cannot let it make a slave of me."

"I don't intend to make a slave of you. I know you cannot be content without a career. But there are things you can do. You can teach music. You can give lessons in dance and song. You can write and produce dramas. There are many things."

Gomer shook her head. "That is not for me to decide. The gods have honored me with a special position. How can I turn my back on that?"

"Is it what your gods want?" Hosea asked. "Or what Jothan wants?"

Her face was stricken. "Please don't say those things. Jothan is my sister's husband. He loves her. He is going to be a father. But he also is my High Priest. That is different. You must see that."

"I see more than you give me credit for," he replied, his eyes blazing. "Do you think I'm blind and stupid? You think I don't know how he feels about you? You think I don't know everything is different since he was here?"

"That's not because of him. It's because I knew what I had to say to you and that this would hurt you." Her voice dropped in a helpless plea. "I know you still don't understand."

"I understand you want another man."

"Oh, that's not true. I love you. I want only you. After all this time, when our love has been so good and so perfect, how can you say that?"

"Then prove it, by not going."

"Never go?" she gasped.

"Never," he asserted.

Gomer took a deep breath. Then a strange light came into her eyes. "All right," she said. "I will give up my gods if you give up yours." At Hosea's pained expression, she rushed on. "Don't ever go to your study again to worship and pray. Don't ever go to the Temple in Jerusalem. Don't ever call upon God Jehovah. You give up your God and I'll give up mine."

His voice was full of misery. "My God does not require anything that would hurt either of us."

Gomer's eyes filled with tears. "I don't want to hurt you."

Moving at the same time they came into each other's arms. Hosea whispered against her hair, "Then please, do not do this thing."

Gomer cried as he held her, as he pleaded, and their love-making that followed was of a quiet desperation. Something sweet and wonderful seemed to have ended and neither knew how to recapture it.

Several days later when Hosea came in from the fields, she was not there. A servant reported that Gomer had gone to visit her relatives. But he knew. This was the time for their festival.

He looked in on Jezreel, who was sleeping. Dinner was something he engaged in automatically. It was tasteless but he went through the motions.

Walking out back to the garden, he thought of the past year. She would think of that tonight and know she could not be with another man. Tonight she would probably present an offering of thanks. She might even dance on the steps, and suddenly the image of it all was as vivid as if it were happening.

I should never have let Jothan come into my house, he thought. To stop the thoughts, he put his fists to his temples and shut his eyes. No, no, no. He would not suspect his wife. He would not accuse his wife. She would do nothing to jeopardize their love, their family, their home. She would not. She could not.

She would not stay at the temple. She would see everything differently. Anytime now she would come home. It would all seem different now that she had known Hosea's love. He must believe that and not go looking for her.

Afraid of that thought, he hurried into the house. He looked in on Jezreel and prayed that Gomer would remember her child. Remember she was a wife and mother, and remember all he had told her about idols and the one true God.

The night drew on. She didn't return and he didn't think he could stand it. He went onto the roof to look and to watch. She couldn't know what she was doing. She couldn't. He went to his study and cried out to God, but found no peace. He tried not to think about her, and Jothan, and the activity taking place. He tried to pray but his anguish increased and his anger rose until he could bear it no longer, and finally the night was spent. Exhausted by the night's emotion, he fell into a restless slumber and awoke when the sun was high. In his crumpled clothing and unruly hair, he went to the nursery.

The baby was asleep. The servant said he had slept well, had his breakfast, had been bathed and had just fallen asleep. When the servant could not keep the concerned look from her eyes, he knew Gomer had not returned.

Going into the outer court, he walked restlessly around the stone wall, then went to the wooden gate, opened it and walked outside. He stared as she came into view in the bright sunlight. She looked radiant and rested. There was a happy glow about her. She was at peace.

Gomer slowed her pace when she saw him. The questioning in her eyes turned to fear when she saw his unkempt appearance. Never had she seen him like that. He looked as if he hadn't slept at all.

As she tried to pass him and enter the gate, he reached out and grabbed her wrist. "You do not come and go at will, without a word." His voice was deadly.

"I told you," she said.

"That was days ago."

"But you knew." She lifted her chin defiantly.

Despite her struggle, he would not release her. "You look awful," she said finally.

"How do you expect me to look?" he barked. "Knowing my wife is off spending the night with another man?"

"He is not a man," she replied defensively. "He is a god."

A deadly stillness, like some great dark shadow, seemed to invade his being. This must be some terrible dream. A nightmare. She did not deny it, only that Jothan was a man. He was her High Priest. He was her god. "And did either of you consider your husband?"

"Of course," she answered immediately. "Jothan and I talked about whether or not you would join me in temple worship. I told him it was not likely."

"And he was greatly saddened by that!" Hosea retorted.

"No!" she replied defiantly, her eyes beginning to reflect the same fire as his. "Of course it doesn't matter to him."

"Of course it doesn't matter to him," Hosea mimicked. "Except he was very glad. That's his business. He gets paid, in more ways than one, for taking other men's wives."

Gomer wrenched her arm away from his grasp and covered her ears with her hands. "Oh, please. You and your wicked mind are making something degrading out of what is sacred and beautiful. I won't let you. I won't let you."

"Wicked mind?" he snapped vehemently. "Because I don't want my wife sleeping with another man?"

"If you don't want me to be with another man, then come to the temple as my partner. You will see I do not prefer Jothan to you. I never have. I never will. But I want to worship my gods. And that is what my gods require."

Because he was silent, and the expression in his eyes had ceased to be deadly, she thought perhaps she had reached him. He seemed to be listening.

"We don't ask that you give up your God, Hosea." Her voice was low and pleading, sweet and musical. "Bring Him with you. You don't have to worship my gods. You can worship your God in our temple. We can be together. Don't let this destroy what we have."

Had, he was thinking. He felt as if this were some stranger standing before him, pleading with him to submit to her idolatry and immorality.

"Come and you will see. I don't want another man. Only you. Please. Try it."

Suddenly it was as though a light flashed on inside Hosea. A sick smile crossed his lips. "All right," he said, not taking his eyes from her. "I will go to your temple. I will show you what I think of it. Let us confront your great High Priest and let him tell me to my face that he feels nothing for you except a sacred duty. Come on!"

"No." Gomer pulled back, sensing something terrible in him.

He grabbed her wrist, rushed to the stables, took a whip, and she feared he would beat her. She had to run occasionally to keep up with him as he paced through the wooded brown hills where God had given him the word to marry Gomer, plunged down the incline and past the well where their love first began, and neared the village where he had once proudly walked with her.

His eyes lit upon the gleaming structure on the hilltop and stopped so abruptly that Gomer almost fell. "Look," he shouted, pointing the whip toward the temple. "That is what you call a thing of beauty, but it is ugly. It is where you have destroyed our marriage that God ordained. It is there you have broken the vows you made to me and before God."

His angry voice attracted the attention of passersby, stopping activity along the dusty streets. "Please don't," Gomer whimpered as he strode toward the temple, followed by a growing crowd.

"It is there," he shouted, pointing to the structure up the hill, "where babies are murdered, innocent young girls are turned into prostitutes, all done in the name of religion."

When he reached the top he faced the village below and shouted, "I will enter through the front portals of this house of abomination." It was as if he dared anyone to try and stop him. No one moved. Turning on his heel, he again grasped Gomer's wrist as he charged through the doorway. His breathing was raspy, his coarse linen tunic wet with sweat from his armpits to his waist. With red face and blazing eyes he glared at the interior. "Where is the god you spent the night with?"

Gomer cringed against the onslaught of his words. Her hoarse whisper was barely audible through nervous lips. "He is never here this time of day," she lied frantically. "He never comes here the day after a wor—a ceremony."

With a sneer, Hosea whirled around. "These are your gods," he spat in disgust. With a mighty sweep, he sent the whip singing through the air, thudding against golden objects, crashing them to the floor. "Images!" he shouted, striding about the room, leaving no shelf untouched. "Objects! Fashioned by an Israelite craftsman!"

With heaving chest, Hosea bolted up the carpeted steps three at a time and struck out at the great statue holding the golden platter. It didn't budge, but stared out with blinded eyes, a silent, grotesque mouth smearing its face and a bulging belly protruding beneath its bare chest. Hosea's arm was lifted, ready to strike again, when his gaze registered upon the velvet couch beneath the object. The taste of acid in his throat was making him physically ill.

Slowly his arm fell to his side. His clenched fist opened and the whip slipped from his hand. "O God," he breathed. "What kind of man am I, to be reduced to fighting stupid, inanimate objects?"

Like a man defeated, with slumped shoulders and deep furrows above troubled eyes, he walked down the steps and away from the temple without a further glance toward the cowering frame of the woman he had loved so dearly. With heavy heart, trembling lips and glazed eyes, he cared not that the villagers stared at a man whose energy had been spent, whose fury had been left behind on the temple floor in the form of broken objects. He felt as if his heart was one of them.

Jothan knew that if he did not tell Rizpah, she would hear it from other sources and his silence would give her cause to be upset. "He was like a wild man," Jothan said, "taking a whip to the god on the platform as if he could knock it over. Of course, he didn't make a dent in it. Some of the smaller statues were demolished. He smashed them to the floor. The entire temple was a terrible mess."

Rizpah's eyes widened. "You were watching?"

"I was in the inner chamber. I heard the commotion and started to go out when Beniah came rushing in. He informed me that it was no time to make an entrance. We, like cowards, shut and barred the door."

"That wasn't cowardly, Jothan, but the sensible thing to do. And to fight him would only cause a greater scandal."

"I doubt it could be any greater." Jothan's face was livid with anger. "He shouted for all the village to hear, about idolatry and abomination to God. He's a crazy, wild man. I thought he had more sense, more control."

"He's a gentle, good man, Jothan. You know that. You know how devout Hebrews are about their God. And you know how he loves her. There is no mistaking that. You saw how happy they were. And now, what happens to them? Now that she has—"

"She has done nothing but worship her god," Jothan shouted.

"But you know how he sees it. To him, you are a man and she is a woman. That's it, Jothan. And you wonder why he behaved the way he did? It is a miracle he did not take the whip to you."

Jothan drew himself up and paced angrily. That thought had crossed his mind while he stood behind the barred door.

"Of course," Rizpah said, watching him carefully, "there may be a solution to all this."

Jothan stopped pacing and looked at her, puzzled. Rizpah took a deep breath before continuing. "You could banish her from the temple."

A look of disbelief crossed his face. "Banish her? What on earth for?"

"Well, that is done when a worshiper causes a disturbance, Jothan. When marital problems or jealousy arise. It's for the good of the other worshipers. You have done it before. Surely you have not forgotten."

"This is not the same." Jothan turned from her. "I cannot see banishing a temple goddess who has been trained all her life. Why punish her because of an irate, jealous husband?"

"It might save her marriage if you did," Rizpah argued.

Jothan's shoulders rose slightly and a muscle twitched at the side of his jaw. At last he replied, "I cannot interfere in their marital problems, Rizpah. What they do in their marriage is up to them. It is not for me to save or break it. It is my duty to perform as High Priest of the temple and maintain my own marriage."

He came over to her, smiled and placed his hands on her shoulders. His voice was gentle. "My greatest concerns are that a healthy child will be born to us and that you can then return as High Priestess. You know how important these things are to me, don't you?"

"Yes, I know, Jothan," she said honestly.

"You know I love you," he said.

She nodded. She did know that. But she also knew the importance to him of his other obligations. She knew he was a commanding, vital leader in the temple. He was an exciting man, with a presence and demeanor that commanded response from his audience. As a dynamic, virile man, it was his duty to be matched with such a woman. She knew that she and Jothan reigned magnificently together during temple worship. And she was all he needed, usually. But now she was with child. She needed this child more than anything. And a baby would be good for Jothan. But it would be awhile before she returned to the temple.

"What will you do about Hosea?" she asked.

Jothan shrugged. "Post temple guards, if necessary."

So she knew he would not banish Gomer. As if sensing her thoughts, Jothan drew her near and kissed her lips. It was a tender kiss, loving. But it held no passion. That would have been spent last night at the temple, with Gomer.

"Why are you crying?" he asked gently.

"For Hosea," she replied quietly. "He thinks you are just a man."

"He is a stupid, jealous fool," Jothan responded, filled with a sudden anger again. "He is the one who is just a man. We shall see how he fares when he pits himself against the gods. They will not easily accept his having desecrated the holy temple. He would not listen to reason when we invited him into our midst. The gods will deal with him accordingly. It is my sacred duty to influence Gomer away from his blasphemy against our gods.'

"Of course," Rizpah replied. It was spoken like a true High Priest. Jothan always had the right answers. But her tears did not stop. She rebuked herself and told herself she must pray more.

Gomer's sobs would not be silenced. Two days passed and she cried unceasingly. Hosea would not go to her. When she entered the nursery to see her son she would burst into tears again. Hosea stayed mostly in his study. He could not sleep in his own room, for when he entered her sobs became louder. Then she would wail at him from her bedroom, "How could you humiliate me so? How could you call me such dirty names for all the world to hear? How can you take what is beautiful and make it ugly? Why have you stopped loving me?"

Hosea finally went up onto the roof to escape her sobs and accusations. "O God," he cried out on his knees, lifting his pain-filled eyes toward heaven. Then he found that he could not pray. He did not know what to ask for, what to seek. He felt only the darkness of his soul, and the terror was more devastating in his separation from his God than it was in his separation from his wife. Finally, feeling a terrible weight on his shoulders, he spoke aloud. "My violent actions were my own," he admitted. "And they accomplished nothing. I don't know what to do. I will be silent until You speak."

He spent the night lying on the mat on his study floor, no longer trying to make sense of his life that seemed torn to shreds, but listening for a word from God. He did not bother with food and drink. Unless some word came from God, his life was in vain.

He dozed intermittently as he waited through the night. A

faint pink ray of dawn was creeping through a crack of the closed shutter when a spark of reasonableness crept into his mind. No longer did he attempt to discard unpleasant thoughts or reject honest speculation. God was speaking through his own mind. He rose to open the shutters to bright sunlight, then sat at the desk and wrote the words on parchment. It was therapy for his soul and a message to God's people.

In a personal way he saw why God was so much against the Canaanite religion that bound people's hearts and minds. As he wrote, the indictment fell not on objects and unassuming pagans, but on the priests of Israel, and even himself, for not speaking out boldly about God and what He required. God's chosen people had failed to tell the world about the one true God. The Israelites knew the message of Jehovah but did not share it. The heathen knew only what they were taught to know. It was the Israelites who were the abomination; they were the worst offenders. It was they who had turned from God and become idolaters. It was Israel, and the priests, who had sinned.

When he saw the stain on the parchment, Hosea realized that the wetness had come from his own eyes. God did not hate Israel, nor the priests, nor the heathen. He loved them. He did not want to destroy them; He wanted to save them from evil and eternal destruction. Hosea knew it was because of his own love for Gomer that he could understand God's love for Israel.

As the sun rose higher in the sky, Hosea revised and perfected the thoughts that now manifested themselves on parchment. He rose from the chair, stretched to rid himself of the weariness and stiffness of his weakened body. Holding onto the window casing, he allowed the sun to touch his face and realized the weight was gone from his shoulders. A wry smile touched his lips, but with disturbed eyes he turned from the window, suddenly aware of his unkempt appearance and physical needs. He rejoiced that he knew what he must do as a servant of God, but he was concerned that he was not sure what he must do as a man and as a husband.

Hosea bathed, changed, played with Jezreel, had his dinner, and was standing at the doorway between the inner and outer court when a servant came to the top of the stairs. "Oh, sir, come quickly," she urged.

Turning, Hosea saw the fear on her face. The tone of her voice prompted him to take the stairs two at a time. Gomer lay crumpled on the floor by her bed.

"She tried to get up and just fell," the worried servant said, wringing her hands together.

Hosea lifted her from the floor and onto the bed. "Bring something nourishing," he ordered. Then he lay her back on the pillows, brushing her hair back from her face.

The servant brought soup and warm milk. Hosea forced it through her lips. She tried to shake her head but was too weak to protest. He came back every hour and repeated the process. Finally color came into her face and she opened her eyes. "Why don't you just let me die?" she asked weakly.

"Don't say that," he said.

"If you don't love me, I can't live. I don't want to," she moaned.

Hosea took her in his arms. "It's because I love you that I behave so stupidly. I cannot think reasonably when I think of you. . . ." He buried his face in her hair and cried.

Gomer clung to him desperately. "Don't stop loving me," she pleaded.

Hosea was not angry with her anymore, but there was a restraint about him for the first time since their marriage. It was the next day that he spoke to her calmly.

"Your family is not welcome here anymore," he said deliberately, without malice. "You have taken your stand concerning your god. It is against everything I hold dear and sacred. I will no longer pretend to you, your family or anyone how I feel about my God and your so-called gods. I will not be silent before your family. You are never to ask me to worship your idols. Is that clear?"

Gomer nodded. It was a long time before she spoke; then the words were so quiet he barely heard them. "Would you have married me had you known I would go back to the temple?"

Hosea was thoughtful before he replied. "I believe it was within God's will that we marry. And I cannot imagine not having married you. No, I can never regret my marriage to you because of what you have given me: your wonderful love, a child, a home life that was unsurpassed. No, I cannot regret that." He spoke with a solemnity that sounded as if something were over.

"But we still have those things, Hosea," she said softly and put her hand on his. "We have our home, we have our child. I love you the same and you say you love me."

He turned his hand over and tenderly held hers, then looked at her and smiled. But there was sadness in his eyes.

Chapter Sixteen

Jason had heard reports about Hosea's angry demonstration in the temple of Baal and that his marriage to Gomer was in trouble. When he came to visit Gomer and Hosea, he noticed right away the deep sadness in his friend's eyes. But Hosea and Gomer greeted him warmly.

"Before I do anything else," Jason said, "I want to see the baby."

Gomer laughed. "You'll be surprised to find him a very big boy since your last visit. He's trying to say words now and thinks his fingers are the most marvelous toys."

"You two go on to the nursery, Jason," Hosea said. "I'll see about some refreshments and meet you on the roof."

"He's asleep," Jason whispered when they walked into the nursery.

"He sleeps soundly, so you don't have to whisper," Gomer said, looking proudly at her son.

"You're very fortunate," Jason said.

"I know," Gomer replied, then looked at him. "You and Marabah should have a child."

"We would love to," he replied seriously.

"I'm sorry I didn't get to your wedding, but this one was just an infant then."

"We understood that," Jason said, "and are still in awe of the wedding gift. Those golden goblets are masterpieces."

"My father is a master craftsman," she replied.

"Shall we join Hosea on the roof?" Jason asked.

Gomer hesitated and he thought she was about to cry. Then she smiled. "I have some things I must do. You two have much to talk about."

"When will you come and see our new house?" he asked.

"Soon, Jason. And thank you," she replied as he left the room.

Gomer stood looking at her sleeping child. How nice if she and Hosea could be friends with Marabah and Jason. But she could not go to their home without a personal invitation from Marabah, and she did not think that would be forthcoming. If Jason didn't already know what had happened, Hosea would tell him. She hoped he wouldn't dislike her. Sighing deeply, she walked slowly to her bedroom and stared at the goddess Ashtoreth. "Bring us happiness again," she whispered.

Jason joined Hosea on the roof where cakes and cups of goat's milk were spread on a table. There were only two cups. Obviously Hosea hadn't expected Gomer to join them. He sat down, picked up a pastry and sampled it. "Great," he said, then took a drink from the cup.

"How are the newlyweds?" Hosea asked him.

"It's a good life, Hosea," Jason said seriously. "One couldn't ask for a better wife than Marabah."

"Does that surprise you?"

"No, but it's a little frightening to be married to someone who does everything so well. It's only been a couple of months, but I can see the pattern there. I spilled oil on her polished floor only yesterday and she merely said, 'Clean it up!' Not to me, to a servant."

They both laughed.

Jason had asked Marabah to marry him a week after Hosea's wedding. She had expected it and said yes. Asa and Deborah were delighted, but not surprised either. A man, and a priest in particular, simply did not show the kind of attention to a woman in public as Jason had done at the wedding, unless his intentions were serious. While waiting the customary year, Jason had built a house for Marabah at the other side of the village, on property Asa had given them as a wedding present. Jason didn't think Marabah would want to live in his house in Jerusalem where he and Sarah had dwelt. Marabah was a proud woman.

Marabah's gifts were many. She knew how to run an efficient household, show proper devotion to her husband, make him feel as if he were the head of the house, and win the admiration of priests, rabbis and their wives through the quality of her elaborate dinners. Jason's pride in his wife was obvious.

Then Hosea sighed. "You've heard, of course," he said finally.

"If what I've heard is true, then you must learn to control your temper," Jason warned.

"Yes, I know that," Hosea replied, sounding somewhat repentant. "I admit I was not in control. I must not let that happen again."

Jason looked at him steadily. "Was it so unexpected?"

An ironic smile lay on Hosea's lips. "I suppose I was egotistical enough to think I could compete with their gods," he said. "And I should not be so surprised. Since I was sure God wanted me to marry her, I felt certain she would turn from her pagan ways." He shook his head in desperation. "I was wrong. She has not changed. Sometimes I think it would be easier for me to change, rather than her."

Jason felt his pain, but did not know how to advise or console. "Do we give God a time limit, Hosea?"

"I don't know if I can live with it, Jason. Anything else, murder even, would be easier to deal with. Irreparable damage may already have been done to our marriage. I blame her. She blames me." He gestured helplessly.

"Do you still love each other?"

"Amazingly, yes," Hosea replied. "That in itself is a miracle, after the things we've said to each other. But the issue is so deep. It involves everything we each hold sacred."

"Have you learned from this experience, Hosea?" his friend asked quietly.

Thoughtfully Hosea stood and walked over to the wall. "I will admit I was tempted, Jason. Not tempted toward accepting those idols, but desperate enough to compromise, to pretend for the sake of our love and our home that I should go to that temple to keep her from other—gods. But I won't. I can't. I know that with a certainty. Despite my love for her, my allegiance to God is stronger."

He turned troubled eyes toward Jason. "I hope I am not being overly confident, but I feel I have made an irrevocable decision to hold onto my God. I believe this even though I don't understand what He is saying to me. It seems almost that He gave me a priceless gift in my wife, and then He asks me to choose between her and Himself." He shook his head despairingly.

"From what you've said, Hosea, you did choose. You did not compromise. She is here. You still love each other. But if you go on like this, you will destroy each other." Jason paused, wondering how to inspire confidence in his friend. "You were going to win her over to God."

"Jason, surely you know this is my first desire. I mean, if she said, 'I'm sorry, forgive me,' I would be more than eager to do that. But her commitment to her gods is not something of the past. It's an ongoing thing and will continue. I have to find a way to stop it."

"As I see it, Hosea, there are only two ways you can go."

"What are they?"

"One is for you to say, 'I divorce you.' Then it's over. You give her over to the pagan gods without a fight."

The astonishment in Hosea's eyes told Jason that this way was not even a consideration. "All right," he resumed. "Then you continue what you started when you married her. Remember your determination to show her your God and persuade her to forsake her false ones."

"Jason," Hosea said slowly, "I don't think you understand what's involved here. Our most intimate times. The expression of our love. How can I willingly share this with another man?"

"I don't know, Hosea. But you have to go one way or the other."

"What has been accomplished, Jason?" he asked helplessly.

"More than you think," Jason replied. "As a man, you won her love. Her gods did not keep her from loving you or choosing you. As a man, you made your wife happy and brought a son into the world. As a man, you have been tested and passed that test by putting God first in your life. As a man, you have introduced an idol worshiper to God Jehovah. Those are not defeats, Hosea. Those are accomplishments. Now do you forget that and turn from her?"

"But how can I forget her unfaithfulness, Jason?"

"I don't know. If you have tried and failed, then—" He paused. "You're back to the first possibility."

"You know, Jason," Hosea said warmly, "you don't talk like a priest."

Jason laughed. "Would you be talking with me if I did?"

"No," Hosea admitted. "Because I know what they would say and I would not like it."

Jason looked tenderly at his friend. "Hosea, our darkest moments are what make or break us. You know how I felt about Sarah's death. I felt God had abandoned us both. I could not understand it. But I have learned that I do not have to understand everything. I believed at that time I would never even look at another woman. Now I am married again and appreciate my wife more perhaps because Sarah and I had such a wonderful relationship. All the little things I never knew Sarah did for me, I now know because I lost her. I am not glad Sarah died, but I am glad for the things I've learned because of it. We have to learn to get beyond our pride, our emotions, and hold onto our faith that God is working in all situations even when we don't understand it, even when we feel He is far from us. Be open to Him, let Him speak, let Him work in you, don't shut Him out."

"I suppose everybody knows what has happened," Hosea said, his voice low.

"Was it not you, Hosea, who told them?"

"I wasn't trying to lay her sins before the world, Jason. There was my own hurt and jealousy and anger with her, but most of all I was enraged at our kind of world in which such abomination is allowed to exist. When I am able to be objective, I see that the blame does not lie with her, nor with them, but with . . . us."

Hosea's voice lowered as he continued reflectively. "I do try to look at it from Gomer's point of view. My father says I am being called a wild man, a madman who has disgraced a temple goddess in the eyes of her family, her religious leaders and her community. She is living with that, too."

Jason watched him carefully. "That is not all they say about you," he said quietly. "These accusations have been hurled at others before you. Some are saying that God Himself is speaking through you."

Hosea sat staring at his hands clasped in front of him. "I am afraid," he whispered.

"To be favored of God is never easy," Jason continued. "It demands much. Can you turn away from it?"

Hosea shook his head. "I do not want the ridicule and criticism that comes with telling others about their sins. I do not ask for or seek that. But if God gives me a word for His people, I will not turn away from it."

"You know I'm behind you all the way, Hosea," Jason assured him.

Hosea looked at him with gratitude in his eyes. "That means everything, Jason. Would you like to go to Jerusalem with me this weekend? I want to meet with the priests and suggest we make another appeal to King Jeroboam to forbid our people from erecting altars to the pagan gods."

Jason agreed and they made plans to stay at Jason's house in Jerusalem. As he bade his friend *shalom*, he remembered that this trip would take place during the new moon festival. He wouldn't know if Gomer went to the temple of Baal. Then he looked out toward the darkness. That was not exactly true. He would not ask her, but he would know.

Before dawn Hosea rose to eat a hearty breakfast with Jason, then went to the roof and watched the soft glow of morning light begin to cover the Jerusalem hillsides. It would be a warm day with many people in the streets to buy and sell while the weather was good. Soon the cold, wet winter would settle in, bringing a deluge of rain.

Hosea's eyes traveled down to where the glorious Temple stood majestically in the midst of the city. He recalled the spot where he had watched in awe, many years ago, when Amos had climbed the steps, clad in coarse goat's skin, and spread his arms out to the people. His voice of authority had rung out a warning over the valleys and hills: "Hear the word of the Lord."

Today would be Hosea's turn. With excitement and apprehension, his mind reviewed the words that God had laid upon his heart and mind. When Jason put a hand on his shoulder, the two left the house and made their way through the village streets.

They walked down the winding path, past stone and mud houses built into the hillsides, past olive and fig trees and grapevines bereft of their fruit until another season. As they neared the heart of the city, a clamor reached their ears. Merchants were readying their stalls and booths for customers, much of their produce coming from Beeri's farm on which Hosea had labored during the harvest. Doves cooed in their cages. Traders argued prices. Carts and donkeys clattered over the cobbled streets.

Since Hosea and Jason had been familiar figures in the city of Jerusalem for many years, they soon attracted a following. Hosea greeted people warmly, but his thoughts were on what Jason had said to him during breakfast: "People will question you about your personal life, Hosea. Only tell them what God has given you to say."

Hosea knew this would be hard to do. He recalled how Amos had silenced questioners with a loud voice and withering stare that dared anyone to dispute his word from God. But Hosea was not sure how his own message would be received, or even if anyone would listen.

They stopped by various booths to talk to people on the way to the Temple. One man drew Jason aside. "Was it true about Hosea and the temple at Bethel?" he whispered.

"Come and hear," Jason challenged him. By the time they

reached the Temple courtyard, a large group of merchants, citydwellers, priests, women and curious bystanders were milling about the courtyard as the white-robed Hosea stood by the altar beside Solomon's great Temple.

Hosea's gaze scanned the crowd. He was surprised at the sudden silence when he faced them. There was an air of expectancy in the onlookers—some with anxious faces, others like Asa who seemed embarrassed, some of his friends and priests who appeared skeptical, a few who whispered, a few who sneered, and his friend Jason who seemed to have something in his eye.

"Hear the word of . . ." he began, then after a pause, added, "the Lord." A sense of power replaced the trembling he had felt when he first stood facing the crowd. He spread his arms out in front of him, toward the people. His face muscles relaxed, and his troubled brow smoothed out in confidence as his eyes traveled from one person to the next and his strong voice carried throughout the courtyard.

"O house of Israel, why do you reject My words? Why do you ignore My priests and prophets who have been chosen to teach you, to direct your paths? If you do not change your ways, your land will soon mourn; all who dwell in it will languish, and the beasts of the field and the birds of the air and even the fish of the sea will be taken away."

Jason stared in wonder. Many times he had heard Hosea speak out forcefully on one issue or another, daring to take a stand against priests, and even the king. But today was different. Hosea was not giving forth his opinion. He was speaking the mind of God. The crowd and the priests sensed the difference, and stood hushed by the authority in his words.

As Hosea continued his message, there were sharp rebukes for everyone listening. But Hosea closed his remarks with the reminder that the Israelites were God's chosen people. "Rejoice, you people," he thundered, "for God loves you. Put your trust in Him and He will be your shield and defender. Obey His laws and He will bless your lives in a thousand ways."

Those in the audience who remembered the stern Amos felt Hosea's message a welcome relief. Who could quarrel with a prophet who reminded them of their privileged position in the world, and of God's love for them?

Hosea descended the steps and his eyes met Jason's. The furrowed brow indicated to Jason that Hosea was uncomfortable and displeased with himself. A ripple of murmurs traveled throughout the crowd; most of the remarks that reached Jason were approving. Friends soon surrounded them, and the High Priest invited Hosea into his chambers.

"He asked me to teach our young men, interpret the prophesies to them and instruct them in copying the Scriptures," Hosea told Jason later in the day.

Jason nodded, fingering his beard reflectively. He glanced over at Hosea as they walked along the city streets. "You've accomplished much for one day. No one hurled insults. No one threw stones. No one even questioned you. They did not threaten to put you outside the city gate as they did with Amos. Perhaps that's what disturbs you, eh, Hosea?"

Hosea was striding along the path that now led up the hill. He slowed down, a grin tugging at the corners of his mouth. "As you well know, Jason," Hosea said, "that message today meant no more to the people and the priests than when a stern father reprimands a wayward child while reminding him of his love."

"Was it not God's message?"

"Yes," came Hosea's quick reply, his eyes flashing. "And one of the most difficult things I've ever done."

"Difficult?"

Hosea snorted, looking down the street past the olive trees

to the city wall. "You know me, Jason. I have been more emphatic and forceful while talking with a group of priests who agree with me." They both laughed.

"Today's talk was more difficult for me than my act of violence in the temple of Baal. I did not speak my mind today because I had to learn to be disciplined by God. He commanded me to speak with gentleness and love. It is almost painful for me to allow God to use my mind, rather than yielding to my own passions and emotions."

Jason watched Hosea with a renewed sense of admiration. "Perhaps," he murmured, "God's message to the people is one of love."

"It always is," Hosea replied, then added, "at first."

During the following months Hosea raised no questions when Gomer said she was going to see Athalia and would stay overnight, or that she wanted to see Rizpah and take some of the clothes that Jezreel had outgrown, or a toy. They pretended it was the same as when he said he was going to Jerusalem overnight, or to talk with Jason, or to see his parents.

They had good times together in the evenings when it was wet and cold outside and they had the roof shut off. Often they met in the sitting room in the late afternoon to be with Jezreel who could now sit, clap his hands, laugh and try to talk. They loved the way he shouted when Hosea held him high in the air. And how entranced he was by Gomer's singing! Jezreel would stare adoringly at his mother's beautiful face, then reach up to touch her lips with his fingers.

That reminded Hosea of how he had felt when she had sung so often to the children at the well before they married. One night after their eight-month-old boy had been put to bed, Gomer looked at Hosea with a special glow in her eyes.

"I am going to have another baby," she said softly.

"Wonderful," Hosea responded immediately, taking her into his arms. They hugged and kissed and laughed together. It seemed that they had recaptured the first year of their marriage.

In late August, on a very hot afternoon, a baby girl was born to them. She came in screaming, her face red and her mouth open. Black hair was down to her ears. Nothing anyone tried would quiet her until she was ready to be quiet.

"Stubborn," Hosea said and laughed one evening when even Gomer's singing would not soothe the child.

"She certainly doesn't have the sweet nature of Jezreel," he said.

"I've heard they're all different." Then she smiled slyly at Hosea. "But I see the way you look at her. I think even her crying delights you."

Hosea laughed. "I'm sure I love my children equally, but this little girl has quite stolen my heart. She is . . . so much like her mother."

Gomer felt a tug at her heart. It wasn't often he said things like that any more.

"I think she will be a terrific singer," he added.

"She's already a terrific screamer," Gomer retorted.

Gomer was glad Loruhamah had captured her father's heart. The tiny girl responded to her father in a way she did not respond to anyone else. He could hardly wait to hold her and play with her after a day's work or several days in Jerusalem. When Jezreel was restless, Gomer's singing would soothe him. Not so with Loruhamah. Only her father's arms did that. They needed each other.

Hosea gave permission for Athalia, Diblaim and Rizpah to see the new arrival. They were not invited for dinner. But Rizpah could not come and Gomer's parents stayed only a short while.

"I've been having pains in my chest," Athalia said, placing her hand over her heart. She did not look well.

Gomer soon began her daily dancing practice to keep her body trim and supple. Rizpah had returned to the temple months before as High Priestess. Gomer visited often with Athalia and would go to the temple to offer sacrifices. Her gods had made her fertile and she was grateful. She offered prayers nightly to the golden statue of Ashtoreth.

Chapter Seventeen

When Jezreel was almost two, he was such a bright little boy that Hosea told Gomer one day he wanted to begin his son's religious education.

"When we sit down to eat, we will remind him where our livelihood comes from," Hosea said firmly. "We will make it plain that God Jehovah is the Creator and sustainer of all life. In the evening, after his supper, you and I will instruct him in the ways of God Jehovah. There will be no mention of a pagan god, or idol, or any image. Not while I am here. Not while I am away. Is that clear?"

Gomer listened silently, drew a deep breath and looked at him coldly. "Hosea," she began, "I have told you before and you seem to forget. I am not a Hebrew woman. I will not be coerced. You must not forbid me things. I am not your slave."

"You are my wife," he said plainly.

"Yes, but I don't think it means the same to us."

"You are right," he answered. "But I do not speak of this lightly. It is no longer just you and I. We have children."

They said no more.

The following day after Jezreel and Loru had their dinner, Loru was put to bed. Hosea, Gomer and Jezreel walked in the woods for a while and Hosea talked about God. They returned and went onto the roof. Jezreel became restless.

"Would you like to tell him the story, Gomer?" Hosea prompted, expecting her to refuse.

In her musical voice, Gomer told the story of Noah to Jezreel, who listened intently. After the servant took Jezreel to bed, Hosea complimented her. "You did a fine job. You're a loving mother and I am proud of you," he said.

"I do not mind doing this," she replied. "Your God is a wonderful, majestic God. I like talking about Him. Of course, I don't know as much as you do."

"How did you know that story so well?"

"It's one you told the children a long time ago at the well."

"And you remembered?"

"I think I remember every word you ever said," she said. "I loved you so." She paused and looked at him, her voice lower. "I still do."

He came to her immediately. "And I you," he said without hesitation. He began to kiss her and she gasped delightedly. "My beautiful dove," he whispered against her neck and hair. On the roof, with the stars as their blanket, their lovemaking was fulfilling.

Hosea was afraid of his emotions. He knew, since the time he had knocked down the statues in the temple, to what extent of violence he was capable. To guard against his temper, he showed no surprise when Gomer began to visit Rizpah again, and when she went to see Athalia, whom she said was not well. But he was deeply angered the day little Jezreel looked up at the sky and after Hosea asked who made the stars he replied, "Baal."

Gomer held her breath, but Hosea said nothing. His face became as stone and a veil passed over his eyes. It stayed during the next weeks as he fell into a silence. Gomer was afraid of it. They continued to go through the motions of family life as he had said they would do.

Loru was six months old when the news came that Athalia had an attack.

"We must go," Gomer said.

Rizpah and Jothan were there when they arrived. Diblaim was so upset he could hardly function. Doctors said the attack was probably due to Athalia's inactivity after retiring from her temple duties. She had grown heavier and was not exercising.

"I will help all I can," Rizpah said, and hesitated as if she wanted to say something else but decided not to.

"We think Rizpah is with child again," Jothan finished for her.

Hosea turned and walked from the house. He did not need to stay in order to see the pain in Rizpah's eyes because of her husband's obsession with Gomer, or Athalia's knowing glances, or Diblaim's unconcern. He had forgotten not only Jehovah but everything else except for Athalia and his gold.

Hosea waited for Gomer outside and they walked home through the hills. The beauty of the evening went unnoticed. They both were disturbed. Gomer made an attempt at conversation. She was angry with his silence. If he were not so stubborn, everything would be beautiful. "I'm glad Rizpah is having children," she said. "She's so pleased."

"I'm sure she's a wonderful mother."

"You like her, don't you?"

"Yes," he answered frankly. "I think she and I have a mutual understanding."

"Maybe you prefer her to me."

"Nobody," Hosea emphasized, glancing toward her. "Nobody prefers Rizpah to you."

Gomer said no more and neither did he. She started up the steps to her bedroom when they arrived home. "I want to talk to you," he said.

They went onto the roof. She sat across from him.

"Why do you only go to the temple when you can be the High Priestess?" he asked suddenly.

She stared, unprepared for such a question. He continued, "You were trained to be an assistant. Yet you have never served in that role."

"I'm not really needed unless Rizpah can't be there. Many of the temple staff can act as assistants."

"Is that the reason? Or is it Jothan?"

"Of course it's not," she denied quickly. "Jothan is High Priest. He is just a representation of the gods. But rather than let you think that I go only because he's there, I will tell you. I have been many times. To offer sacrifices. To instruct the assistants in dance technique. And you know I was composing a musical production for a festival. I have not confined my activities to . . . Jothan."

"Could you not worship as well with the temple assistant?" he asked coldly.

Gomer felt uncomfortable. "Beniah . . . frightens me," she said.

Hosea did not like what he was doing. He did not know what to do. Seeing Jothan again—his smug, self-satisfied attitude, standing quietly in the background, not angry, just waiting—Hosea began to feel the hate and anger and jealousy. It kept going through his mind that Jothan was winning. He was sure of himself, and why not? He had been the one to train Gomer in the art of lovemaking when she was but a child.

Hosea felt that anything he said simply drove Gomer further away. He had tried to make her see his side and failed. He knew she would go back to the temple. Rizpah had known. They all knew. They knew he could not change Gomer any more than she could change him. Jason had been right when he said there were only two ways to go. He had tried the second way. What else was there to do?

His voice sounded foreign even to himself. "Have you ever tried the rituals without the incense and the wine? Have you discovered how sacred the act would be with a dirty, toothless old man as your partner? Would it be as fulfilling as with your sister's husband?"

"Stop it! Stop it!" Gomer screamed, putting her hands over her ears. "Why do you insist upon making it ugly? During the ceremony he is not my sister's husband. He is a god."

"Why do they pick the most beautiful girls? Why not the homely? Are only the beautiful ones acceptable to your gods? Or to the priests?"

Gomer stood facing him, feeling desperate. "Of course it wouldn't be the same with the ugly. When you sacrifice to your God, would it be as meaningful if you used a pig's liver instead of a spotless lamb? Would you feel as giving if you offered weeds instead of grain? No. We offer the best, just as you do. We make our services as beautiful as possible."

No amount of reasoning or discussion would alter what had been part of her for twenty years. He had tried before. He had explained about God and His commands. She accepted what she wanted of Jehovah and rejected the rest.

"You are jealous," she accused him. "You are jealous of my gods."

"Yes," he admitted. "Your desire should be to your husband and not to other men—or, as you call them, your 'gods.'"

She paced angrily in front of him. "You want to make a recluse of me. Well, I will not cover my head as if I'm ashamed of my hair. I will not hide my body as if it is degrading. I am proud of being a woman and I will not be hidden away."

"I do not want you to hide your beauty. I want you to use your talents and abilities. If I had wanted a Hebrew woman, I would have married one," he added, his brown eyes expressing pain. "I want you at home with me, with the children, to worship the God I worship, to build a home and family. I want us to enjoy each other, to laugh and sing. The act of love is wonderful. But your religion makes a spectacle of the body. It is sensuality."

She shook her head. "You're so wrong. To keep it private is to deny the good in us. Can't you worship your God your way, and let me worship mine my way? We've been doing that, you know. And with time, you'll get used to it."

That was part of what he feared. He sat with his hands on his face. Yelling and screaming would do no good. No amount of words, calm or otherwise, did any good. "We have children. They are learning. I hoped you would come to understand."

"One of us is wrong, Hosea. I think it is you. You think it is me. But you have to show me something. I can show you representations of my gods. Where are yours, Hosea? This seems like jealousy and selfishness to me. Can't you see that?"

Hosea sighed deeply. "I can see that it would look that way to you. And some of it is. I am a man who loves his wife. I believe you should be with me only. You are not for other men to have and ogle. That's how I see it. But I have failed. I see that, too."

When tears came into her eyes he stood, walked over to her and took her hands in his. "Do you love me, Gomer?" he asked quietly.

"You know I do," she replied.

"All right," he said, his voice pleading. "I am asking you. No, I am begging you, not to go to the temple again to engage in those rituals."

"Begging me?" she gasped.

"Yes," he nodded. "Please, please do not go."

Gomer put her hand to her throat. She shook her head helplessly. "You can't make this a test of my love," she said, her words faltering. "You know—"

"Yes," he said, nodding again. "I know all the arguments. We have been through them time and time again. Now, I want you to understand me, Gomer. And I do not want you to interpret my past tolerance of your activities as weakness."

He took a deep breath before he continued. "I have failed to show you my God. Our love is not enough to keep you from going to your gods. I have nothing else to offer." His voice was shaky but determined, and his eyes held hers in a steady gaze. "So I am ordering you not to ever, ever return to the temple of Baal."

Her shock was reflected in her eyes. Finally she stammered, "You—can't—*order* me."

"Yes, I can. And I am. You did not obey me when I told you not to teach Jezreel about Baal. I will have no more."

Her voice was very low. "You are asking me to choose between you and my gods. How can you? I never asked such a thing of you."

He shook his head. "No. I'm not asking. This is no longer a debate or a discussion. I have not come to this easily or quickly. I have used everything in my power to persuade you. I have nothing more. No more tolerance. No more patience. No more words."

He stopped suddenly, then roughly pulled her to himself. He could not look at her and say it. "If you go again to the temple and engage in those rituals, you will no longer be welcome in my house."

There was silence. They did not seem to be even breathing. "Repeat those words to me," he said finally and stood back from her, tears on his face. "Repeat it."

"If I go to the temple"—her breath came in short gasps—"I

am no longer welcome in your—not our!—home." She jerked away from him and flung herself onto a couch, sobbing.

Hosea turned and left the roof.

Gomer did not know how long she cried, but finally realized she was very cold. She walked to her bedroom and stood before the statue of Ashtoreth, then picked it up and held it to herself. Ashtoreth would not let Hosea do such a thing. He was just angry and jealous because he had seen Jothan. He would reconsider and know he couldn't ask her to choose between him and her gods. Her gods had given him to her in the first place. She and Jothan had asked the gods and they caused Hosea to propose marriage. Then, after she returned to the temple and he was so angry, she had asked Ashtoreth to bring him back, and it happened that very night. The gods would not let him do this.

She stopped her crying and said a prayer to Ashtoreth.

The following day Gomer was not distressed, but looked as if she knew some secret she was not sharing.

For several days Hosea spent most of his time in his study. It was to God alone that he could pour out his heartache. He refused to speak against his wife to another human being—not even to Jason. But in his study he could pray, speak the words aloud, write them on paper, and they seemed like therapy for his troubled soul.

There was no healing for his heartache, nor was there a lessening of the pain he felt as a man. When he spoke with God, he was able to look beyond the human factor and pray for Gomer, whose sins were against not only him but herself, and whose soul was in danger of eternal damnation. He feared her life was so filled with wine, incense, music, dancing and sensual desire that she would quickly move further and further from him.

"O God," he wailed aloud. "How can I stand and speak in

Your name to priests who may have delighted in the same ritualistic orgy as my wife? How can I bear to think of my beloved's soul as eternally damned and estranged from You? What can I do? Where did I fail to show my wife the true, living God? And now my son is being influenced more by his mother than by his father." With bent head, Hosea wept bitterly.

Although God did not give him a satisfactory answer, Hosea felt a kinship with God, who was agonizing over Israel as Hosea agonized over Gomer. It was becoming easier to recognize and yield to that stillness, that quiet, that permeated his surroundings when God had a special message for him to deliver to Israel. But it was not easier to deliver that message.

After three days of seclusion in his study, Hosea journeyed to Jerusalem, and was reminded that God didn't seem to care if the weather were cold and wet. A prophet dressed in coarse clothing and heavy wool, his face chapped from the cold, his hair rumpled in disarray and his voice shaking in the wind, Hosea shouted warnings with a finger pointed at the people rather than palms outstretched. He was not as welcome as was that honey-tongued orator in white robe who had appeared months before. Many listened for a while, then walked away. Merchants in the marketplace pretended not to hear. Doors and shutters closed. One priest shouted at him, "It's easy for you to tell us not to go to the temple of Baal. You have Baal in your own home."

It was difficult to ignore such gibes. But Hosea was determined to say what he felt God was saying. He pointed at the priests in the temple courtyard. "You are the wisest men in Israel. You are our religious and political leaders. You are the judges. You see the injustice, bribery, false dealings, money passed from hand to hand rather than keeping the laws of man and of God. There is murder in the streets. There is adultery. Sex orgies taking place in the name of religion. What are you doing about these abominations to our God?"

Angry cries arose from the crowd as Hosea plowed on. "You know how Baalism has spread. Not only in Bethel, but at the shrines in Gilgal, Mizpah, Shechem, and yes, right here in Jerusalem. God is not blaming the pagan. He is blaming His chosen people, in His favored spot in all the world. He is blaming you and me right here in our land. The warning is clear, men of Israel: sow the wind and you will reap a whirlwind!"

Knowing the king was in the Temple, Hosea had asked for private counsel with him. He was not surprised when the king appeared at an entrance during his speech. God had given him a word for the king. "Only one alliance can save Israel," he thundered. "An alliance without God's signature on it is as valuable as a broken pot, as tasty as unbaked bread, as reliable as poisonous weeds growing in a plowed field. When wickedness is planted, the harvest will be bitter fruit. So I urge you, plow new fields. Plant righteousness. Sow your seeds of devotion to God. Cultivate justice. And reap God's blessings."

As a sprinkle of rain began to fall, Hosea ended his message. "God is suffering over us. Don't you know how much He loves you, and how you are breaking His heart? He cannot share His Kingdom with idols. He cannot share you, His beloved chosen bride, with Baal. You are breaking His heart, just as an unfaithful wife breaks the heart of her husband. But if you repent, God will forgive you."

A great sob welled up inside of Hosea and his lips grew silent. With head high and carriage straight, Hosea turned away to walk into the Temple to keep the appointment with the king. The wetness on his face was more than rain.

Several days later Gomer said she was going to her mother's. She was going to stay for a couple of days, for Athalia was worse and unable to leave her bed. Rizpah's pregnancy brought with it a morning sickness that did not leave until afternoon, so Gomer was needed with her mother. "You can manage without me?" she asked.

"We have before," Hosea replied quietly.

The next night Gomer had not returned and it was the night of the new moon festival. Hosea decided to go and see Athalia for himself, but when he passed the village he did not turn at their house. He went up the hill and stood outside the temple doors.

But only for a few seconds. Gomer, looking like a radiant, beautiful, seductive goddess in a diaphanous gown interlaced with gold threads, was dancing on the steps in front of the idol. When she twirled around, the gold threads gave her the appearance of being the goddess Ashtoreth herself. Jothan, in an apparent alcoholic ecstacy, reached out his greedy hands for her.

Hosea turned and walked slowly back home. He did not feel the murderous impulse he had thought he would feel. Walking past the village toward the well, he recalled how she had said her gods had brought about the profusion of brilliant flowers that surrounded them on the hillsides and the valleys. It was almost time for the latter rains again. At the temple of Baal, they would be defeating the death that had enveloped the earth during the winter. They would also be heralding the season that would bring the profusion of spring flowers and fertile fields.

But for Hosea, the next two months would bring nothing but rain.

Chapter Eighteen

Hosea expected Gomer to return the next morning, which would be her usual procedure, but she did not come. It was late afternoon when she appeared. Hosea met her in the outer court.

"I . . . don't feel well," she said, putting her hand to her head. Hosea grabbed her as she began to fall. He picked her up and took her into the house and up to her bedroom. She had fever. "Bring cold towels," he instructed.

"I think I'm pregnant again," Gomer said as he washed her face. "I was terribly sick this morning."

"Let me know when you're sure," he said.

She did not feel well during the next week. They were eating dinner when she told him she was reasonably sure.

"You may stay here until the baby is born and you feel well again," he said blandly. "Then you will leave."

The bite of food was halted halfway to her mouth, which remained open as she gazed at him. He rose and left the table, his food almost untouched.

Gomer knew that Hosea never said anything he didn't mean. But she would have six or seven months to change his mind. Then an icy jolt of fear ran down her spine. What would she do without him? How could she manage the children?

Surely he would be reasonable. He loved the children, even if he no longer loved her. He could not do this to them.

But she did not try to dissuade him, hoping somehow that he would forget he had said those words. A baby boy came two months early, after a difficult pregnancy. They named him Loammi. The heat of summer caused her great discomfort and she coughed steadily before the child came. Much of her time was spent in bed or in the shade on the terrace. Hosea busied himself with supervising the bringing in of the crops.

Athalia had another attack and this time did not recover. Unable to attend the burial service, Gomer grieved for her mother. Her only comfort during those days of fear and illness was Jezreel. Though her two small children grew more adorable every day, Jezreel was special to her. As the summer heat lessened and the coughing finally ceased, Jezreel often slept on the bed with her.

After the baby came, Gomer learned she could bear no more children. The small infant boy soon began to grow healthy and strong. It took longer after this pregnancy for Gomer to regain her strength.

Gomer thought Hosea looked tired, but he had worked hard all summer and during the harvest. After a hard day's work he would spend an hour teaching the children. Sometimes he worked in the garden, allowing Jezreel to help.

Two months after Loammi was born, Gomer was herself again. One night when Hosea said, "Let's look at the children together," she wondered if it were possible for them to return to some kind of reasonable relationship. For a long moment Hosea stared at the sleeping children, then suggested they go to the sitting room to talk. Gomer went on ahead while Hosea stopped to give instructions to a servant.

When they sat down, Gomer looked at him questioningly. "Are you ill?"

He did not answer the question. "The time has come for you to leave," he said stonily.

"Leave?" she gasped.

"There will be a horse and cart waiting for you outside the gate. Take any of the servants you want. Anything else you want. I will send money."

Gomer slowly rose to her feet. "You can't mean this," she said, staring at him disbelievingly. His eyes were troubled but set. He looked tired and ill.

"You would let your jealousy do this to us? To our family?"

After an interminable silence he spoke. "We've been through it all before. There's nothing more to say."

"You chose your God above me. Why can't I do the same?" she cried frantically.

"You have," he said. Fury was on his face. "Go to your god. I'm only a man."

"Please don't do this," she wailed.

"I warned you."

"But I didn't believe you really would. I—I thought you loved me."

"I did."

"You don't? Anymore?"

He didn't answer but turned away and put his hand on the doorway to still the trembling.

"All right. Have it your way!" she shouted and ran from the room. He walked toward her as she stopped on the stairs. "I'll leave," she yelled. "You will never see me again. You will never see the children." As she raced down the second floor corridor, he followed, his face a mask.

Gomer ran to Jezreel's door. It was closed. She tried to open it. "The door, it's barred," she said. "Why is the door barred?"

"The children will stay with me."

"No," she said, shaking her head, her eyes wild. "You can't

mean that." She ran to Loruhamah's door. Then Loammi's. Then she came back to Jezreel's door and began to pound on it. "Open that door," she screamed. "You hear me? That's my child in there. You open that door. Jezreel! Jezreel!"

"You told our servants to do that," she said, turning to face Hosea. "You can't do this to me."

Jezreel, hearing the commotion from within his room, began to cry. Running over to Hosea, Gomer grabbed his arm. "Let me take Jezreel. You know he would not be happy without me. You know that."

"The children will stay here," he repeated.

"Just Jezreel," she begged. "You can keep the other two. If you don't care about me, think of him. Can you do this to him?"

"To keep him from knowing your false gods? To keep him from believing Baal made the stars? Yes, I can do this to him. It is for his ultimate good."

"Please, Hosea." Her voice was desperate and pleading. "Let me take him. I'll tell him about your God. I'll never mention mine. I'll do anything to have him."

"I cannot trust you," he said.

"Think. How would you feel if you could not see Loru? If you could not feel her little arms about you? If you could not hear her baby sounds? If you could not touch her? Love her?"

"How would I feel?" he asked, his look like that of a stranger. "Much as I have felt for the past year or so, I suppose."

Gomer tried to sound calm. "You cannot keep my children from me. You are not so cruel. You're a good man." Hosea only looked stolidly ahead, not replying.

"He's crying for me now," she said desperately. "Won't you let me see him? Just once? Please. Please."

"You will have one hour to get whatever you want from the

house. What things you can't take tonight, I'll send to you." He walked past her, went into his study and barred the door.

In a blaze of fury she beat on the door of his room. "You're a monster to do this to me. I hate you. I hate you." She crumpled to the floor. "Please," she cried, her voice now a desperate whisper.

After a few minutes she got up. "Hosea," she called, but he did not answer. "Is this the kind of God you have? Would He take my children? If so, He is cruel. If He would do this, I would not want to serve Him. Show me your loving God, Hosea, not this monster. Ask Him, Hosea. You want me to know Him. All right. I will. I will do anything you say. I will call on Him. You hear?"

Gomer looked toward the roof. "God Jehovah. Listen to me. I forsake my gods. I will serve You only if You will give me my children. Or just one child. Please. I beg You. I beg You."

She did not expect Him to hear or care. She went into her bedroom and looked at the statue of Ashtoreth, picked it up and hugged it to herself. "Oh, please. Give my children to me. Don't let him do this dreadful thing."

She went back to the door. "Hosea. I cannot live without my children. You want to kill me? I cannot live without . . . you. You know that. I'm begging. I'll do anything. You want me to die? Is that it? Won't you please come out? Don't you want to tell me that you divorce me?"

Would nothing make him respond? She pressed her ear against the wooden door to hear any movement. Silence. "Hosea," she called after a moment, new strength in her voice. "You shouted for all to hear that you consider me no more than a harlot. All right"—and she had to take several breaths to make the words come out. "These are not your children."

There was a movement and faint hope stirred in her breast. Maybe he would open the door and demand an explanation. Surely he would face her once again. But the door didn't open. Yet he must have heard. She beat on the door. "They're not even yours, Hosea. Not yours."

Finally she knew he wasn't going to respond. "All right," she said. "I'm leaving. Since you hate me so much, you will never see me again. But I will not live. This is what you and your God would do to me. I hate Him. I hate you."

Gomer left the house, taking nothing with her. A mule-drawn cart was waiting for her, a servant to operate it. She directed him to her parents' home in Bethel. When she arrived there her father was in his workroom.

"Father, you've got to help me," she said desperately.

He looked at her in confusion.

"Hosea has put me out of the house and won't let me have the children. You've got to help me get them."

He shook his head in bewilderment. "I'm sorry. I have to talk with Athalia. Be a good girl now and run along."

She stared at him in amazement. His mind was gone. What was happening to her world?

She ran out of the house and up the steps to the temple. Jothan was in his private chambers. Rushing to him, she grasped his arms.

"Gomer! What is it?" he exclaimed.

"Hosea put me out of the house," she gasped. "He won't let me have the children. You've got to help me. You've got to help me get them."

"Here, sit down," he said soothingly. He poured her a goblet of wine and handed it to her. She sipped it. "Now," he said. "Tell me calmly."

She tried, but the words spilled over each other. "Is there something I can do legally?" she asked.

"To attempt anything legal would only make matters worse. The court officials would brand you with their narrow thinking and you would have no rights whatsoever. No, you have no legal rights in this situation. You can only appeal to Hosea's better nature."

"He doesn't have that anymore," she wailed.

"After he thinks it over, surely. . . ."

"No. He thinks *before* he acts, not after."

"Are you sure he won't reconsider?"

"I'm sure. He barred the children's doors. If I hadn't left on my own, I'm sure he would have put me out and barred the gate. He will not let me in. He will not talk to me. It's over. And I have nothing. Nothing."

Gomer's long dark lashes were wet against her cheeks. Her mouth trembled with emotion. Her black hair was in disarray. She was utterly helpless and vulnerable. But she knew from the look on Jothan's face that he would take care of her.

"We can appeal to the gods," he said quietly.

"That . . . has always worked, hasn't it?" Her desperate voice held a ray of hope.

"Yes," he answered drily. "It has always worked before."

Chapter Nineteen

I hate you. You'll never see me again. For weeks, months, Hosea could not get these words out of his mind.

Then her statement *They're not your children* had so penetrated his heart and mind that night that he had moved to the window of his room, opened the shutters and looked out upon the brown hills.

"O God," he had moaned toward the trees that blurred before his eyes. No one could take him to such heights, or such depths, as Gomer had. A trembling shook his body. She wanted to hurt him. She wanted to strike out. Then he had to tell himself, that was only natural. Even animals did that when an attempt was made to separate a mother from her offspring.

He would not question the legitimacy of his children, born to his wife in his own home. This was a mother's desperate appeal. That's all it was. Loosening his grasp from the windowsill, he had rubbed his hands together for circulation, then wiped the sweat from his brow.

How long he had stood at the window, he didn't know. Finally there had been sounds in the hallway. A servant was enticing a little boy with cookies to make him stop crying. Then a dank, dark dampness had settled upon everything. She was gone.

The decision to force Gomer to leave his home and their

children came out of intense agony for Hosea. Sticking to it was even harder.

Huldah pled with him, certain that Gomer would not be able to face life at all without her children. "You cannot take everything from her," she said. "You must at least let her see them. You know how she loves them."

Hosea had to turn his back on his mother, shut his ears to her words and walk away. He also ignored the heartfelt pleas that came by messenger from Gomer.

Jezreel, only two-and-a-half, missed his mother desperately and stubbornly resisted Hosea's explanation. Hosea told him gently, time and time again, that it was God Jehovah who made the stars, but Jezreel would stubbornly say, "Baal." Hosea wondered if he would ever be taught differently. He knew it was a way of identifying with his mother, who had encompassed his whole world.

It was Loruhamah who reminded him most of Gomer. She was a beautiful child who touched his heartstrings as no one else could. Her eyes were blue, not violet. Her hair was black. He had to be firm with her, for she had a rebellious spirit and opposed his authority from infancy. "You're like your mother," Hosea said many times. "Your mother is very beautiful. She dances, sings and plays musical instruments. She wears beautiful clothes. She loves you very much."

In the baby, he saw a different side of Gomer. Loammi was a sweet, gentle, submissive little boy who loved everyone and everything. Because he had known his mother only two months, he did not know what he missed.

After weeks of messages, appeals and pleadings from Gomer, all ignored, they stopped. Hosea did not know which was worse—the pleadings he ignored or the silence when they ceased.

For a long time he would not discuss Gomer with anyone.

Jason visited him often, but never approached the subject of Gomer after Hosea had said he would not discuss her. Then one day during Jason's visit, Hosea asked him, "Please tell me all you know of her."

Jason then described the discussions he had had with the priests in the Temple about the outlandish surging growth of Baalism, and the new High Priestess acclaimed as the most beautiful in the world. "She's the High Priest's sister-in-law," they said.

Jason also told Hosea that much of his information came from Marabah, who passed on to him all the rumors. He did not tell his friend that Marabah gained a certain satisfaction from wives who would comment, "Well, what could Hosea expect, marrying a woman like that!"

Both Hosea and Jason were concerned over how many Hebrews were deciding to combine Jehovah worship with Baalism, a self-gratifying religion that took care of the religious, physical and even baser inclinations of human nature. They agreed it was hard to compete with a religion in which one could participate with beautiful young temple assistants and pray to objects, touch their gods and call them by names.

As the months passed, the strain showed on Hosea's face. Gomer was more active in her religion than she had ever been. Hosea kept trying to put her out of his mind.

"I thought after Sarah died that I could never accept another woman in her place," Jason said one evening as the two men sat together on Hosea's roof. "I thought it would be impossible to marry again, Hosea." He paused, then continued, "Children need a mother. A man needs a wife."

They both knew that the marriage would end if he declared himself divorced from Gomer. So few words, which could be said aloud or written, and it would be done. Final! But Hosea shook his head. Would saying the words make it all disappear? Erase everything?

"I have a wife," Hosea said simply, and the subject of divorce was not mentioned again.

Hosea thought of going to her when word came that Diblaim was dead. Then he heard that Rizpah had returned to the temple as High Priestess and that her younger sister was no longer there. Hosea knew if Rizpah became pregnant again, Gomer would resume her office of High Priestess.

Then word spread that if the gods didn't object to their High Priest living with two High Priestesses in different houses, then surely they would not mind if married men participated in worship with temple staff, the sacred prostitutes of Baal.

"What are the priests saying about this?" Hosea asked Jason.

"They want to know if you have a word for them, Hosea. They are asking if you are too timid to show your face. They say for you to divorce your wife and brand her for what she is. They demand that you speak if you have a word from God. They say you cannot be silent in times like these."

"I dare not listen to any voice but God's," Hosea said urgently. "My own voice gets in the way so much. It is more than I can do now to abandon my own will and trust God's and believe He wants me to do what is abominable to my nature.

"I did not want to put my wife out of the house, Jason. I find no pleasure in keeping her from her children. I did not want to cut off her financial support. Yet what could I do? Let her stay and contaminate our children? Go with her to keep her from other men?" Hosea paused, his eyes desperate. "In the same way, I don't like what I must say to Israel. Yes, I have a message to deliver. But I can't see how it will help Israel, any more than my turning Gomer out has helped her. I dare trust only God's voice, and I fear sometimes, Jason, that I am not touched by God but by madness."

Hosea looked toward the stars and smiled grimly at Jezreel's insistence that Baal made them. "God will give us His message. He will tell us that He is abandoning His people, turning His back on us, cutting off our blessings, no longer providing for us. We will call and He will not hear."

Hosea turned again to Jason, asking intensely, "Does God no longer want us? Will He decide never again to have a chosen people? Will He find another race? Another man like Abraham, and start over? Or will He wipe man from the face of the earth and be sorry He ever made him? What is He doing?"

Jason was quiet for a long time; then he spoke softly. "Jacob must have felt much that way when he thought his son Joseph was dead. Where was God? Had God forgotten His promise? Was God not true to the covenant He made with Abraham, Isaac and Jacob himself? The answer is that God didn't tell Jacob He had Joseph safely in Egypt, becoming the most powerful man there, next to Pharaoh. God did not abandon His chosen people. He was making a way to save them from world famine, so that they might survive and multiply as He had promised they would do."

"How desolate Joseph must have felt," said Hosea. "He had been so proud, so sure he was better than his brothers in many ways. Then to have been in slavery and in prison for so many years! There must have been times he felt completely abandoned by God."

"Yes," Jason agreed. "But God was working out His plan for Joseph and His chosen people then. He is still doing it, Hosea. He has spoken in the past. He speaks now. If God were going to abandon His people for all times, without a remembrance, would He bother to warn us? Why would He even speak? Why not just act?"

Hosea looked gratefully at his friend. "You have more faith than I, Jason."

"No," he said, shaking his head. "But what faith I have did not come from blessings received. It came through trials."

Hosea straightened in his chair. "Well, Jason, I have to decide what to do with the children if I'm going to Jerusalem."

"Can't Huldah and Beeri handle them?"

"If they wanted to, yes," Hosea replied. "But my mother says her heart hurts for a mother who cannot even see her own children. She understands why they must be apart, but doesn't agree that I should forbid visits. I'm afraid I cannot trust her in this situation."

"Marabah is not a mother," Jason said. "Perhaps she could be more objective. I'm sure she would love to stay in our absence. She, Huldah and Beeri, plus your servants, could handle the situation."

Two weeks later they went to Jerusalem. Once again Hosea thundered from the platform about the deplorable situations in all areas of Israel's life. He lashed out at those who drifted over to Baalism, especially the priests. "Persist in your evil ways, and God's punishment will fall on you like the thundering floodwaters from the mountains."

While in Jerusalem, Hosea learned that Jothan was now a part of the high council of the High Priests of Baal and had been transferred to the temple in Tyre. Many wondered aloud which High Priestess Jothan would take with him to Tyre. Perhaps both.

Chapter Twenty

When Hosea returned home from Jerusalem, he discovered that all had gone well in his absence. The children were eager to have their father home again. Even Jezreel seemed anxious to please him.

Marabah had taken charge of the household in his absence and developed a special fondness for the children. In the days that followed, she and Jason would come by so that Marabah could surprise the children with a treat. Then she would tell them stories before bedtime while Jason and Hosea talked on the roof.

Marabah had also discovered little things awry about the house that a man would not notice and servants would not take care of unless someone told them to. In the process of tending to these, she could hardly help but remember, as she had remembered many times since the broken engagement, that this house had been built for her. Rooms were filled with children that might have been her own. But in the bedroom that might have been hers, there was no woman but a golden statue of a naked woman standing on a lion.

Late one afternoon Marabah appeared bearing a plant for the garden. Hosea planted it where she directed. When he learned that Jason would not be back from Jerusalem until the following morning, he suggested she might like to help with the children.

After their lessons and the children were put to bed, Hosea asked, "Would you stay for dinner?"

"I would love to," she replied.

They talked of Ephraim, his parents, her parents, even some of the old times when they had had fun together—times that seemed like another world to him. Dinner was pleasant. Hosea enjoyed sitting across from a woman again. After dinner it seemed only natural to gravitate to the roof and enjoy the coolness of the evening.

Hosea felt comfortable with Marabah. "You have a good life with Jason, don't you, Marabah?" he asked with a smile as they sat down on the couch.

"Yes," she said. "Jason is a good man." She hesitated. "Even if he is older."

"Older?" asked Hosea in surprise. Jason was somewhere around forty and in excellent health. His manner was that of a young person.

"Well," said Marabah—and he detected a reticence in her—'it seems I've always been married to an older man."

Only at that moment did Hosea feel a slight uneasiness. Suddenly he realized that the entire afternoon and evening had been most unusual. It also occurred to him for the first time that if he and Marabah had gotten married, this would have been her home.

Hosea stood up and walked over to the edge of the roof. "Older?" he repeated, looking out into the night. "I don't exactly relish the idea that you and I will be classified as older when we're Jason's age. He's only ten years older than we are."

"I know. But he's been married before to a woman who was

ill for many years before she died. I suppose that makes him seem—so mature, or something."

"He's a fine man, Marabah. A good friend to me. He's a priest. The kind of man you always wanted to marry."

This is ridiculous, he told himself. *Marabah, like a sister to me, knows all this.*

She didn't reply to his comments and he did not move. All was silent as she sat demurely, her head high and her hands clasped on her lap.

"You must get very lonely, Hosea," she said softly.

He started to reply that he had a busy life with his business, the running of a household, being the only parent to three lively children. He also had lectures to prepare and deliver, lessons to prepare for the young men at the Temple, friends and family who came to the house. Yet he knew all that would sound hollow at the moment. After his life had been filled with so much, how could he not be lonely?

"I suppose that's why I value friendships so much, Marabah," he said, not looking at her.

His hands trembled slightly. He did not want to think the thought that came into his mind. It wasn't really a thought, but a sort of possibility that had been there, waiting for his awareness, and now it had to be faced. Women were available for men without wives.

What kind of woman could he take? A servant, who would be afraid to refuse because she might lose the job that meant her livelihood? Could he reach out with greedy hands to a woman he would pay to lie with him? Were there any others?

He did not want to feel what he was feeling. He did not want to admit that he would like once again to feel a woman in his arms. How pleasant it would be for someone to care for him that way, someone who would lie in his arms and at least say loving words, whether or not she meant them. It was not easy to admit that he was young and there might never be a woman in his arms again.

Never suddenly seemed like a long, long time, and he wished the word had not surfaced. Of course everyone would understand. People did understand about those things. They were tolerant of a man's needs. And who could blame him? Would God Himself? God understood. After all, He was the One who created man and recognized, even invented, man's need for a woman.

He hardly knew how to continue this conversation with Marabah. He asked inanely whether or not Jason knew she was there with him.

"No," she replied, and he had never heard her voice sound so uncertain. "But he would not mind. He—trusts me."

Hosea spoke automatically. "Of course he trusts you, Marabah. He often speaks of what a fine woman you are."

As he spoke, he was aware that things of the flesh are often more powerful than those of the intellect. He trembled at his own weakness. If honorable, God-fearing Hebrews could be so tempted, then how could one expect more integrity of those who did not know God? When one with God's strength was so vulnerable, what of those who had only their own strength?

He knew that the strength of one's life could be diminished to a frail emotion. And telling someone to choose between emotion and such things as honor, integrity and resolve is like telling someone to choose between the sunrise and the sunset. In a weak moment of temptation, was there really a choice? The sunrise and the sunset were at opposite ends of the noonday heat.

How long he stood there, staring into the never of eternity, he did not know. When finally he turned around, she was gone.

How foolish, he told himself. She was like a sister, and was his best friend's wife. She had been concerned about him because she was his friend.

Marabah returned to her home berating herself for the foolishness of her visit to Hosea's house. She told herself she hadn't really said or done anything out of the way. But she knew what was in her heart.

How often Jason had said, "Look at the parallel between Hosea and Gomer, and God and Israel." He said it in awe, as if that woman could be part of God's plan. She certainly could not see that. She saw a pagan woman who had stolen her fiance away, leaving her rejected and humiliated.

When she had gone to Hosea there was still, deep in the recesses of her heart, an unforgiving spirit, and she sought to take revenge. If she had diverted Hosea's attention, it would have meant revenge on that woman.

She would have liked to hear him say he had made a mistake, that he should never have married Gomer in the first place, and that he wanted her. Just once, to have him say that! And if he had turned to her, then she could have refused him, proud of her strength, and humiliated him. She told herself that because she felt ashamed.

But deep down she knew that's not the way it would have been. She would have responded if he had asked her. Why not? For twenty-four years she had expected to spend her life with Hosea. He had changed. She had not.

In trying to be honest with herself, she admitted that she had delighted in the evening with Hosea, wondering and even pretending what it would have been like if that had been her garden, her children, her dining table, her husband.

Now she asked herself how she could have done such a thing. She knew now what an alien, sinful spirit lurked in her heart, and the awful possibilities that had existed. Now she could look at everything more realistically.

Hosea was, as Jason said, a prophet of God. She was not the kind of woman to be married to a prophet, for many ridiculed him, disbelieved him, laughed at him, scorned him. Some rejected him because of his love for a pagan woman, feeling him weak in abandoning God; while others felt him wrong not to join her in Baalism.

He was talked about constantly. Everyone knew his affairs of life; nothing was private, concealed or secret. She could not be married to a man like that. She wanted a well-ordered life—one of respect. God knew it. God had given her the kind of man she always wanted, always needed; the kind of life she was meant for, trained for and—loved.

When Jason came home the following morning, Marabah met him outside and rushed into his arms with tears in her eyes. Jason had not know her to cry since the night before Hosea's wedding.

"Oh, I need you, Jason," she said. She seemed helpless, different. Usually she was self-assured, going about her daily routine with total dedication and without flaw. It was scary sometimes, for he feared he might fail to be part of the perfection with which she seemed to surround herself. And yet her responses and attitudes toward him were ideal, all that a husband could want. She never refused him her lovemaking, never criticized or nagged.

Somehow now to see her cry made her seem vulnerable, made him feel protective. He rejoiced that she turned to him as a source of comfort. Maybe she did need him after all, for something other than having saved a proud woman from humiliation.

Jason put off going to see Hosea for a while, since he and Marabah seemed closer and he didn't want to spoil it. After several days he asked her to go with him, but she said no, she had things to do. He went on alone.

"Did you hear anything new?" Hosea asked. Jason knew what the question meant.

"Only that Jothan has defintely accepted the position at Tyre and will soon leave. Beniah will take over as High Priest at the temple in Bethel. No one seems to know if the High Priestesses will go or stay."

"Beniah," Hosea said carefully, sudden concern on his face. "Something about that name bothers me, but I don't know what."

Marabah was different during the following weeks. She thought about her relationship with Jason very seriously. She realized she had been afraid from the very beginning that she might fail to meet his expectations, that he might compare her with his first wife and she would be found lacking. She tried to be all that a respected, admired man like Jason deserved.

Although she knew she could not ask for a better man, a better husband, she had grown to accept him and take him for granted. She had thought of them as two people who had no one else, liked each other, and should come together to make a good life and enjoy the companionship each wanted and needed.

They had been married three years now and she had never once said she loved him. He had said it several times, but more flippantly, as when she surprised him with the embroidered vest to wear over his robe and he had delighted in it and said, "Ah, I love you, woman!"

She would try it.

"Jason?" she said as they sat across from each other one evening.

He looked at her. "Yes?"

"Do you ever think of Sarah?" That was not what she meant to say.

He was silent for a moment and a strange look crossed his face. Then it relaxed. "Yes, Marabah," he said slowly. "Not often. But it is good to think of our past relationships, for they help us build better ones. We can gain much by our memories. They help us learn and grow, if we use them properly."

Marabah looked down. She hadn't used hers properly. "You're very wise, Jason."

He waited before he replied, and it did not sound flippant. "I know," he said. "I married you."

"And I—" She paused, and he watched as she drew in a deep breath. "I . . . love you for that."

"Say that again," he demanded, his voice seeming to rumble from him.

She looked up quickly. "Jason," she said in a strangled voice, color flooding her face, for she had never seen him look at her quite that way. A devouring look and a strange smile was on his lips. He rushed over and stood in front of her. "Say it again."

"I love you, Jason."

He pulled her to her feet. Joy was in his voice and on his face. "Now, may I tell you all the things that are in my heart?"

"I wish you would."

He smiled, then kissed her. It was a long time before they broke away.

She smiled at him. "That was an eloquent speech, Jason. I'm glad you told me."

Chapter Twenty-One

It looked like rain again and Gomer was glad. Otherwise she would not have ventured out into the cold, windy day with only a gray cloak and hood wrapped around her, to sit on the stones at the well outside the village. She never went there anymore unless it was on a day like this, when no one else would be around to stare or ask questions.

She did not even look up at the brown, rocky hills, for there was nothing to see. Nothing but wet trees, slippery rocks, sodden slopes, muddy footpaths.

When she finally raised her head and felt the cold rain against her face, she saw the outline of the barren hillsides ahead. She was not dancing now, she was not singing, she was not praying, she was not sacrificing. She was not a goddess now, but the flowers would come out again, too.

She didn't think she ached inside anymore. The feeling had become so much a part of her it was almost undetected—just the heavy weight that never lifted. Most of the time it was a vacuum, an emptiness she had tried hard to fill with wine. It helped some, for a while, but when the wine was gone, the feeling was still there. It never left.

She had thought at first Hosea would reconsider, or at least allow her to see the children. But things had not grown better, they had grown worse. Finally he had even stopped sending money. It had been more than a year since he had put her out of the house. She knew now it was final.

The priests of Jehovah who worshiped at the temple of Baal told Jothan, and Jothan told her, about Hosea's public discourses. He called Israel a silly dove. He had once called her a pretty dove and a sweet dove. She knew. He could talk about Israel all he wanted, but she knew he was talking about her. He had said God would withhold his blessings from Israel so that she would then know where the blessings had come from. Strange—or was it?—how that coincided with Hosea stopping the money for her support.

He talked about Israel prostituting God's love and selling herself to Egypt and Assyria in return for a false security. She had thought that did not apply to her, but now she knew it did. She was selling herself in exchange for a few words that sounded like love, for the warmth of a body to fill her empty arms.

Beginning to feel the rain even through the cloak, she pulled it closer around herself and with bent head hurried toward home. Jothan might come to her tonight. That's all she had now. When he came he looked somewhat like her god she used to have. But he was not a god, and she was not a goddess. Would that mean there *was* no god?

If a god existed, and if he were Hosea's God, then she was more desolate than ever, for Hosea said God had turned His back on Israel. If God didn't love Israel, He couldn't love her, because she was not one of His. And Hosea treated her as God treated Israel. Hosea never changed his mind once it was made up. But then, he didn't need to. He didn't need her anymore. His life was filled. He had his family and friends. He had his home and children. And he had his God, who loved him so much He spoke to him personally.

The rain poured down and the thunder rumbled. It reminded her of another time when she had run home in a storm. As she walked faster, she did not look up at the top of the hill toward the temple. She tried not to think about the past, but when she went inside the house there was nothing to do but think.

She had two servants now, young girls who worked for almost nothing. When the last of her possessions were gone, the girls would go, too. Now they helped her out of the wet clothes and brought a change. They rubbed her skin with oil and brought hot food and warm milk. She thought of another time when Jothan had come to her in this very room as a High Priest and a god. Now he came as a man.

The storm outside made no difference. She did not care that the stones trembled. She would not care if they fell on her. She did not care that the lightning streaked the sky. She would not care if it struck her.

Her hair was still damp when she walked through the house, wearing silk in case he came. She was still holding a golden goblet and drinking fine wine.

She looked around at the empty workroom. Her father's pride was no more. He was no more. Her mother was no more. She would not care if she joined her father and mother except they did not "dwell in the house of the Lord forever," as Hosea's King David had written about. She could not have even that hope. There was nothing.

She remembered the night the tragedy occurred. Diblaim had never recovered from his loss of Athalia. He sat in his workroom and wailed for Athalia and cried to his golden objects and drank himself into insensibility. Gomer hadn't understood at first, feeling he should not be so grief-stricken since he had a home, his worship, his children, his friends, a thriving business. Why did he behave as if he had lost everything?

Only recently did she understand. When one had no god, the other things were not enough. And Diblaim lost his god when he lost Athalia.

She had followed him the night he went to the temple to sacrifice to Athalia. He had climbed the steps to the great golden idol. He moaned and chanted and lit the burnt offering. But the oil spilled on his long loose robe. The flames engulfed him. He began to fan them with his robe in an attempt to put them out, but it only made it worse. She screamed and tried to help but he ran down the steps and outside before anyone could stop him.

Diblaim was writhing in agony in the groves at the back of the temple when she and the others got to him. But he didn't live. The burns were too severe. She had heard his last words, which were seared in her memory: "The Lord God is one God, and Him only shall you serve. Forgive me, Lord." It sounded so much like something Hosea had said.

Why would her father's dying words be something from the Hebrew religion? He hadn't worshiped Jehovah in more than two decades. How could it still be a part of him? How? She knew, of course. It was not easy, maybe impossible, to rid oneself of what had been taught in early childhood. It had not been easy for her, and she wondered if it were not better to have a false god than no god at all. Surely there must be one somewhere who could love her. But who? And where?

She remembered how she had tried to appeal to Hosea; had sent messages, but they were returned or unacknowledged. All efforts to obtain a response from him had failed. All pleadings she made to Huldah had failed. Huldah said Jason could not speak to Hosea of her, either. It was as if she were dead to him.

Remorse had overtaken her and she had even cried out to Hosea's God. She had begged Him, "Let me return, or let me see my children one more time. Or even one child. Just once. Just a glimpse, and I will know You are God and serve You gladly."

But He didn't do it. She had asked Him. She had begged Him. But there was no response. None.

But there had always been one thing that changed Hosea and that was when she appealed to her gods. Hadn't they made him love her in the first place? Hadn't they returned him to her after he had been so angry? Hadn't they caused him to marry her? It was Hosea's God who put her out of the house.

Then she decided that perhaps her gods had been angry because she had not sacrificed to them enough. They had felt abandoned because she had often put her husband and children before them, and had listened and talked about Jehovah. She would repent. She would sacrifice. She would implore and they would once again look upon her with favor and make Hosea at least let her see the children. Her gods would win.

So she had entered into temple activities with a new abandon, giving to them all her hopes and dreams, entreating them, imploring them to intercede in the deplorable situation. No one could have served a god more faithfully than she for the next months, engaging in public and private rituals and service to the temple duties. For they were going to return her children to her. When?

The assurance that the gods would restore her to some relationship with Hosea and the children had already turned to a sense of desperation, even before Rizpah returned to the temple as High Priestess after having her third child. She tried not to doubt, but kept asking why the gods did not do something. The worship became less satisfactory. She could not dismiss Hosea's words that such activity was but temporary pleasure and that God would bring His judgment to bear upon it.

After Rizpah came back, Gomer continued everything except the public rituals, for she could not bring herself to be Beniah's partner. She asked herself why and remembered Hosea had asked the same.

One night during the new moon festival, she did not drink the wine. She had not meditated and allowed the incense to numb her senses. She had not danced, but went coolly, calmly to the temple and watched. Beniah had seen her inside the doorway and had staggered drunkenly toward her, saying that someday he knew she would come to him. She ran away from the temple, down the hill and into her house, and lay sobbing on the bed. She did not want Beniah. She did not feel like a goddess. She felt like a woman who wanted her husband and her home and her children and a god who had more to offer than Jothan or Beniah.

Another time she asked Jothan why the gods did not grant her requests, and he said they were displeased and did not want her to have that Hebrew prophet who talked to all Israel, including the king, against Baalism. But then why had the gods given him to her in the first place? Hadn't they known?

When the doubts came, Jothan said it was because Hosea had poisoned her mind with his insane ramblings. But she thought she would prefer insanity to the meaningless existence that was now hers.

And now she had stopped asking those idols for anything. She stopped asking Hosea's God for anything. She was even glad her children did not have her. They would be better off and she would not try to see them again. Hosea had been right. She was glad her children would not grow up to be like Beniah, or her father, or Jothan. She was glad they would grow up to be like Hosea, and maybe his God would love them, even if they were still so much a part of her.

So she wandered about the house and waited. Finally Jothan came, hurrying, wet, and she laughed as he dried and changed and she sipped her wine. She knew what to say and do to please him. It wasn't difficult. He was the one who had taught her. And she could even feel sorry for him. A man, almost forty, who should be home with his wife and children, was with her because he was not a god, but a man and a slave to his body.

And I? she thought. *No, I am not even that. I am as Hosea said about Israel—a silly dove, selling herself to Egypt and Assyria for a false hope, a pseudo-security. And what did it matter, anyway? It passed the time . . . until what? Until another morning, another day, another night, another evening when he would come again. And pass the time . . . until what?*

Chapter Twenty-Two

It had been two years since Hosea had put Gomer out of the house. Jothan had gone to Tyre and rumor had it that she had gone with him, though no one seemed to know for sure.

When the High Priests of Baal Council met in Jerusalem, Jason approached Jothan and asked if Gomer was with him.

"She is welcome to come here at any time," Jothan asserted, his cold eyes showing his resentment for Jason and what the Hebrews had done to Gomer. "But she is not here now."

"Where is she?" Jason asked.

"Why the sudden interest?" Jothan snapped. "It's rather late to be concerned about her welfare." He turned and walked away.

Jason reported the incident to Hosea.

"And you say she has not returned to the temple rituals?" Hosea asked.

"That information came from rather reliable sources," Jason replied. "And they say she is still living in the temple house below the hill."

"Without an income from me, with her father's gold nearly gone and no income from the temple? How does she support herself?"

"They say," Jason replied, "that Beniah supports her."

Then Hosea remembered. He and Gomer had been arguing

one day when she had admitted that something about Beniah frightened her.

"I'm sure she would not live with Beniah," Hosea asserted.

"What can a woman do without means of support, Hosea?" Jason asked quietly. "Does she have a choice?"

"She made her choices all along."

"No, Hosea. We do not choose everything that comes our way. She did not, either."

"What else could I do?" Hosea asked despairingly. "What can I do now? She must hate me."

Jason said nothing, but watched his friend. Hosea was in one of those desolate, desperate moods that often occurred just before God gave him a dreadful message to deliver to Israel. Many times recently Hosea had said, "I cannot tell them what God seems to be saying. I must not be hearing Him right. It cannot be. He would not let that happen."

God's message stayed on Hosea's mind day and night. He felt he must be misunderstanding it. Perhaps his mind was clouded, because he could not forget the nagging thought of Gomer living with a man who frightened her, and Jason's saying she had no choice.

It was in the middle of the night that Hosea was awakened by pounding on the outside wooden door. He heard Jason shouting. But Jason was supposed to be in Jerusalem.

He rushed downstairs to find that a servant had let Jason inside and he was waiting in the inner court. When Jason told him the reason for his hurried trip from Jerusalem, Hosea knew he had not heard God incorrectly. Nothing could be clearer. He was being shown in a tangible way what would happen to God's beloved Israel. Bounding up the steps three at a time, he prepared to leave immediately in order to reach Jerusalem before sunrise.

Strange, Gomer thought, that it would be at the slave market where she could put a few thoughts together in a sensible way. But there they did not allow her to drink herself into a stupor. They made her eat. They bathed her, washed her hair and covered over the dark bruises Beniah had made. She felt almost human again, even grateful to have risen to the status of a slave. Anything to be away from Beniah.

Now that she had a clear head, maybe she could pull her life back to some kind of meaning, unless the person who bought her was unkind or made detestable demands upon her. Then she would at least have the presence of mind to take her own life. That was a possibility she could look forward to, a ridding herself of nothingness.

Her mind drifted back to the time Jothan had begged her to go to Tyre with him. She had told him then that she could not be a part of the temple anymore. She asked if she could live with him and Rizpah until she found something else to do, but Rizpah would have no part of it. Rizpah hated her now.

"I'll find a place for you to live," Jothan had said. "Then I'll come for you."

Jothan had returned several times. He had found her a place in Tyre. He promised support and frequent visits. But surely, she thought, there must be something, somewhere, more than that. Surely she could find some way to use the talents she once had had. It had been more than two years since she had been able to write music and poetry. Maybe it would not come again. But she should try. Yes, she would try, and if it did not work she would go to Tyre.

During the days that followed she tried to get her life in order, and refused to saturate her mind with wine. Meanwhile, the remaining pieces of gold were spent. The jewels were given in payment for services. When the servant girls left, she was glad for the care of the house since it helped to pass the time. She struggled to write her poetry, but she could not sing. When she tried, she cried.

Then Beniah came. He brought food and cooks to prepare the meal. She was wary, but he was kind.

"Come back to the temple," he said. "Be my High Priestess."

"I cannot."

"Then you must pay for the use of the house," he said calmly. "And the food."

"I have no money."

"No money?" he said, raising his eyebrows over the small black eyes she had always felt were too close together. His lips were thin and red. She shuddered inwardly as he continued, "You could be High Priestess of any temple you choose. There is a place waiting for you on the hill. And you say you have no money?"

She looked away from the gleam in his eyes. His voice remained the same. "You know this house is temple property. The only way you can stay here is if you are part of the temple staff."

She stopped eating and stared hard at him, hating his next words. "But I think we can find a way for you to remain here. I am as adept in such matters as Jothan."

She began to shake her head but he only laughed.

"Do you know how many years I've waited for you? How many years I have dreamed of you, pretending the others were you? No, you do not know. But you will. You will."

And as she rose to leave the room, he followed, laughing, and she was afraid. She had always been afraid of him. So she asked if they could drink some wine. He said yes. She thought it would help, but she hated his awful eyes when he stared at her, waiting, as he had done for years.

She was terrified, but what could she do? There was no one to help. Jothan would come for her someday but he was not here now. Servants were blind, deaf and dumb when they were paid to be. She thought they had gone by now anyway. And where could she run?

When he came to her, she tried to fight him off, but it was to no avail.

After that he came often, bringing food and wine, oil for the lamps, linens for the beds, silk for her clothes, replacing household items that had been given away or traded for food. And still Jothan did not come. After a while, she learned that her fighting only made Beniah laugh in his evil way and incensed him further. He had abused and debased her and the only way she could face herself was to be in a continual drunken stupor.

"First you fight and then you are impassive!" he exclaimed one night in exasperation after his abusive passions had been spent. "But I have always determined that someday you would be mine. Mine!"

He strode from the house. When he did not return for several days, she entertained a faint hope that he had tired of her, that he had given up believing she would ever respond to him willingly.

When the officials came, demanding payment for the rent on the temple house, demanding payment for the food, wine and other items Beniah had brought, she was glad she could not pay. Glad she would be sold as a slave. But she had not taken into account Beniah's warped mind.

When the slave market in Jerusalem opened the next morning, and before any other buyers arrived, Beniah came for her. Then she knew why he had allowed her to be brought to this place.

She had resisted him, angered him, remained impassive to

his advances. He had said that someday she would be his completely. Now he would buy her and she would be his slave legally. No one could do anything if he beat her or debased her. The sound that came from her was a low moan as she turned to face the wall and began to slowly sink down beside it, for her knees would not support her any longer. This was the end. She could not, would not go back to Beniah.

Hosea had taken a horse to get to Jerusalem as quickly as possible. When he arrived at the slave market there was another horse there—a fine one with a purple cloth draped over it. The reins were studded with jewels. Pushing the curtain aside, Hosea rushed in.

Beniah looked surprised. Gomer was huddled in a corner as if trying to shrink into the wall. She was dressed in slave attire, a coarse, short linen tunic draped over one shoulder. Beniah's hand was on her bare shoulder.

"Get your hands off her," Hosea's voice boomed.

Beniah's surprise turned to terror at the look in Hosea's eyes. He began backing away when Hosea grabbed Beniah's golden staff from the table. Hosea slammed him against the wall with the staff at his throat.

"Help me," Gomer whispered. He could hardly hear her above his rage.

"Is this Beniah?" he asked.

"Yes."

"What is he doing here with you?" he asked, but did not take his eyes from Beniah, whose own eyes were popping with fear and inability to breathe. Saliva began to dribble from the sides of his mouth.

"He had them bring me here so he could buy me as his slave. Please don't let him do that."

Beniah's eyes pleaded and he slowly stretched out his arms,

as if in surrender. Hosea removed the staff. Beniah rubbed his neck.

"Apologize to her," Hosea thundered.

Beniah wiped away the saliva with the sleeve of his priestly garment. When a sneer crossed his face, Hosea's fist shot out and made contact with his jaw. Beniah lost his balance and fell against the wall. Hosea grabbed the front of his robe and stood him straight again. "Apologize," he ordered, murder in his voice.

"I—" he began, and his voice became lower. "I apologize."

"Is that good enough?" Hosea asked Gomer.

"Yes," she said, nodding her head weakly. "It's all right. It really is."

"Get out," Hosea ordered Beniah.

"But this gentleman bought her," the seller said, coming in as Beniah hurried out the door.

"Where's the bill of sale?" Hosea asked roughly.

"Right here," the seller said, pointing to a paper on the table with money on it.

Hosea tore the bill of sale into pieces. "Give him his money back and make another bill of sale for me."

The seller nervously did as instructed.

Hosea took coins from his pouch, signed his name and the seller put the seal on the bill. Gomer walked out behind Hosea. Neither Beniah nor his horse were to be seen.

Hosea mounted his horse. She could not look at him. "Come on," he said brusquely. He reached down and pulled her up, then blinked back moisture that was filling his eyes.

She sat sideways on the horse in front of Hosea, while he put his arms around her, holding the reins. Tears streamed down her face. They rode through the main streets of Jerusalem and past the Temple for everyone to see. She knew she should feel humiliated, dressed as she was in slave attire, but how could she be more humiliated than she had already been?

What was Hosea thinking? She dared not turn around. What greater wrong could a wife do to a Hebrew man than she had done? What would he do with her? Where would he take her? In one sense it hardly mattered, since he had saved her from Beniah. But they seemed to be headed toward his home in the brown hills.

Then she remembered something she had said two years before. After he had put her out of the house, she had begged Hosea's God to give her one glimpse of her children. If He would do that, she would serve Him. But she had meant for this to happen right away. Because it hadn't, she thought He hadn't heard or cared or perhaps didn't even exist. Could she have been wrong?

Her heart beat faster. Through her tears she whispered, "The children?"

Hosea's face looked stony. He had not changed expression since he had confronted Beniah. She had never known this side of him, except— She recalled the time in the temple of Baal. Yes, that had been similar. That was when he had begun to stop loving her.

When he spoke his voice was hard. "Our children," he said, looking past her to guide the horse, "are well."

That was all he said. So of course he would not let her near them. He had not wanted her near them two years ago, and she was in much worse condition now.

Chapter Twenty-Three

After putting the horse in the stable, Hosea led Gomer to a lounging chair in the shade of the trees. The sun was high and hot. She said nothing, afraid she might awaken from what must be a dream.

Hosea went into the house and soon a servant came with a cup of cool milk, which she drank, then lay back and in a little while dozed off to sleep.

When she awoke it was late afternoon and an older servant woman sat in a nearby chair. "Would you like your dinner out here?" she asked.

Gomer stared at her, then looked around warily. Yes, it looked like the place where Hosea, in her dream, had brought her. The place that used to be her home. She didn't answer and the woman did not pursue it, but acted as if nothing was unusual.

In a while the woman went into the house, and before long servants came out with trays and dishes of simple foods she knew were nourishing. Previous times flashed through her mind when her dinner would consist of hard bread, or only a bottle of wine. Then there were the delectable dinners Beniah had provided. She hated them, for she knew what would follow. Now, she wondered, what was Hosea going to do with her? He had left her in the courtyard. Should she stay here? She did not know.

When the servants asked if she wanted anything more, she didn't reply. She didn't know what to say. She was a slave, yet the servants were attending her. But didn't that prove it was all a dream? She lay there until darkness brought with it a chill. The older woman came out again. "You should go inside now."

Gomer didn't know if she should obey. But she was a slave. Would a servant have authority over a slave? Hosea should have given her instructions.

"We've drawn your bath," the woman said and helped Gomer shed the coarse tunic. The silky bath water felt good to her skin and she washed gently over the bruises. One of her lovely nightgowns that she had left here two years ago was laid out for her. She did not protest, knowing this could not last.

Following the servant, she went into the bedroom that once had been hers. The bed was turned down.

"Where is he?" she asked.

The woman did not ask who. She replied immediately, "He said that while you are recuperating from your illness, the children will stay with their grandparents. He has business in Jerusalem."

Gomer lay back on the pillows.

"Is there anything else?" the woman asked.

"Could you—" Gomer began hesitantly. "Would you leave the lamp burning?"

"If you wish," she answered, and left the room.

Gomer lay staring about the room. Her eyes stopped on the statue of Ashtoreth. Why hadn't he thrown it away? Her eyes went to the doorway that led to Hosea's bedroom. She was perplexed. She did not understand his bringing her here and leaving with the children. But, of course, she was in no condition to see the children. Perhaps the servants didn't know she was a slave and were mistakenly treating her like the mistress of the house.

Almost an hour passed before she allowed herself to look toward her own bedroom doorway that led into the hall and to the children's rooms. Her heart grew noisy in her chest, and she took several deep breaths to quiet it, but it didn't help. Finally she turned back the covers, slipped out onto the floor and walked toward the children's rooms. The doors were open.

She went into Jezreel's room first. When she touched the bed where he slept, her heart began to hurt. There was a great throbbing in her throat but no tears came. The hurt was too deep for tears.

There were different objects than she remembered. When she left, he was two-and-a-half years old, toddling and beginning to put words together to make sentences. He would be four-and-a-half now, a big boy. He would not remember her. Then she felt the wave coming.

She had known it once before when she had been taken as a small girl to the sea. A giant wave was far in the distance. It began to roll closer and closer until finally it crashed onto the shore, overwhelming her, dragging her back with it. Diblaim, knowing the danger, had grabbed her in time. She had been fascinated, though, and unaware of the danger. It had been so powerful she could not believe it. And now she felt that wave again.

She picked up the little blanket from his bed—his blanket. She brought it to her face. His smell. A little boy's smell. Her boy. Her loving baby. And the wave broke. It came and it receded and it came again. And with it came the terrible wailing that could be heard throughout the house. "Jezreel, Jezreel," she sobbed.

A long time passed before the calming of the sea, and it left the shore barren, empty, clean.

The older servant had harbored some very hard thoughts against this woman who had so wronged that good man of God. But now, after hearing her brokenhearted sobbing and seeing her lying face down on the bed, still clutching the blanket, her heart softened. She could feel some of the ache this woman felt. She had lost a child once, through death. The feeling was akin to the sounds this woman had made and her heart went out to her. She covered Gomer, for now she lay in an exhausted sleep. She left the lamp burning so that if Gomer awoke, she would not be in the dark.

The people stared in horror as Hosea, dressed in sackcloth and his head covered with ashes, walked through the streets, headed for the Temple grounds. They followed, muttering, "He's insane. The prophet has lost his mind."

Many of the priests felt the same way, but a few like Asa and Jason grew fearful of the dreaded message God must have laid upon Hosea's heart.

Hosea was not one for sensationalism, but in his sorrow, and for the purging of his own soul, he knew this day must be remembered and the message must not go unheeded.

"I no longer have pity for My people, says the Lord of hosts," Hosea began his sorrowful message. "The day of punishment is coming. Israel will lie in ruins. God wanted Israel's love, but was given burnt offerings instead. The fortified cities will be no protection from God's fire that shall burn down the palaces and cities. There will be famine. Not enough grain, or olive oil, or wine. Israel will lie desolate, barren, weed-infested. Israel is like a plant whose roots have dried up. The people will cry out to the mountains for cover, but there will be no safety. They will have nowhere to turn."

When Hosea paused, the High Priest could constrain himself no longer. "Surely, Hosea, this is conditional. There is more. Will not God give Israel another chance to repent?"

Hosea wished he could say the message was conditional, that the people still had another chance, but he knew, as God did, that another chance would make no difference. The people had not stopped sinning. The worship of idols increased daily. Social, political and religious injustices flourished. Immorality abounded.

"I will punish Israel for her past sins, says the Lord," Hosea continued. "War will sweep the cities. They will cry out, but God will not hear. And"—he paused, for this was the most difficult part—"Israel will be taken into slavery."

Hosea turned his streaked, ashen face toward heaven and closed his eyes. He had the appearance on this day of a haggard old man. It was he who was the cloud in their blue sky. It was he who had become the storm in the midst of their calm. It was he who brought a disturbance on this quiet, warm, spring morning.

And it was resented. How dare he speak like that? The murmurs became louder.

For a moment Hosea had been lost in his own thoughts. He could not deny the parallel between his chosen bride and God's beloved Israel. His beautiful dove, in slavery. And now it would happen to God's people. What was to happen after that, he did not know.

The shouts began to register. He lowered his head and saw a burly, robust man step forward, holding a stone. The man shouted, "It's blasphemy to make such accusations against God and Israel." Nods and murmurs and shouts followed.

Hosea lifted his arms for silence. "It is I who have an accusation to bring against Israel, says the Lord. The chosen people have made the Lord angry. They will be punished.

Like a leopard, like a lion and like a bear I will attack, says the Lord. Israel will be torn to pieces and devoured. Then who will Israel turn to?"

The people waited for an answer. It did not come. Hosea wished he could tell them, but he could not. That thought, like a shudder, brought a tremor throughout the crowd. Hosea must be wrong. He had to be wrong. Without God, who could Israel turn to?

Hosea always stayed at Jason's house while in Jerusalem. Five days later, he returned home. Gomer had already eaten and was walking in the garden when she saw him enter the house and walk out to the terrace.

When he sat down at a table and began to write, she thought he did not know she was in the garden. He didn't look her way. She had often accused him of wanting her to be a slave. She hadn't really meant it, or even been serious about the word. Now she was his slave, legally. What he would expect of her she did not know, except slaves had to obey their masters.

But she would do anything to be able to stay here, even if her duties were to wait on the servants or clean their rooms, and even if he never spoke to her. If she could just see him as she did right now, sitting in a chair, thinking and writing on a tablet.

Why did he want her to eat properly and gain weight and be strong and healthy? That's what the servants said his instructions had been. What did he have in store for her? He was good and kind, she told herself, but he had not been kind when he kept her from the children. That was cruel. He could be cruel.

She stayed in the garden a long time, then began to feel tired and wanted to sit down. But she was reluctant to go over to the terrace where he sat. For a while she leaned against a tree, then sat on a bench. It began to get dark.

The servants came out and lighted the lamps around the terrace. Hosea laid aside his tablet and sat looking out toward the hills. Gomer felt he would probably sit there all night. There was much she would like to say to him, but did not know how, or if he would allow it.

Finally, when she hoped it was dark enough, she walked back on the garden path and onto the terrace, staying close to the wall that surrounded it, headed toward the house.

"Gomer," Hosea said, without looking toward her. That was the first time she had heard him speak her name in over two years. Her first impulse was to run inside the house and hide from him. Another was to run to him and beg him to forget that the past two years had ever happened. But she could do neither. She was bound to go to him. Perhaps he would tell her what he expected of his newly acquired slave.

How wonderful, Hosea thought, *to have her here, walking in the garden.* But he had to face facts. She was not here of her own free will. There was a barrier between them that had begun to be built long before she left the house two years before, and he wondered if there would ever be a way to get around it.

For a moment he thought she wasn't going to come over to him. Then the hesitant figure approached slowly. She was not as wan and pale as she had been when he brought her from Jerusalem, but still she would not look at him.

Getting up, he moved a chair next to him. "Sit down," he said, and they sat opposite each other.

"Why did Beniah want you as his slave?" His words were more blunt than he had intended.

Her lips trembled before she answered. "I suppose to take from me the last remaining speck of pride I had left. In his demented mind, I would then belong to him legally, although I could never in any other way, except—except—"

"The bruises," he said, interrupting what she found so difficult to say. His hand reached out toward the black and blue marks on her arms that were turning to a sick yellow. "Did he do these?"

She drew back instinctively when his hand came toward her. Tears rolled down her cheeks as she nodded.

She is afraid, he thought, *even of me.*

"And he's the one who was frightening to you a long time ago?" he asked after a considerable silence.

"Yes," she whispered.

"I'm sorry," he said, "that I did not remember sooner. Or take your remark more seriously."

Her eyes quickly met his. Just as quickly she looked down at her fingers entwined together on her lap. Her black lashes touched her wet cheeks. "I thought you had forgotten everything about me," she blurted.

"Did *you* forget?" he asked quietly.

"Would I be like this," she asked with bitterness, "if I could forget? If what I lost did not haunt me day and night, would I be in this humiliating condition?"

"But you have many abilities, Gomer. Could you not forsee your financial plight and take students, or make some of the golden ornaments your father taught you to make? Surely something?"

She shook her bent head. Words came between sobs. "One cannot sing and dance and write music without a reason. I did not have one reason. Everything important was taken from me. I had no home, no parents, no husband, no children"—she paused before saying the worst—"and no gods."

Hosea wanted to believe that, but knew she was at a desperate point in her life. Desperate people often said whatever necessary for survival.

"Why did you stop taking part in temple activities?" he asked. "Was it because Rizpah returned as High Priestess and you did not want to be an assistant?"

She was quiet for a long moment. "It was a combination of things that probably started long ago when you talked with me at the well," she answered at last. "There were questions in my mind that I refused to think about. I expected my gods to bring me the happiness I had here. That did not happen. I fought against seeing my religion for what it really was. It had been my whole life, the most important thing in my life. To lose one's gods," she sobbed, "is to lose everything. And then—"

She stopped a minute, taking the linen handkerchief Hosea handed to her, wiped her eyes and nose, and continued, "Before Beniah came, I thought I might be able to do something with my life. After he came, it was too late. I could do nothing. There was nowhere to turn."

"Didn't you realize I would have helped you out of that kind of situation?" Hosea asked.

"I knew you had helped other people. But I also knew you had turned your back on me. No, I did not know you would have listened to me or helped me."

He hated what he had to ask. For the answer might tear his heart from him again. "Would you prefer to be in Tyre, rather than here?"

It took a long time for her to answer, as she tried to control her convulsive sobs. Hosea guessed she was wondering what kind of life she could look forward to in his home. He did not know any more than she did.

Finally she said, "I'd rather be here."

Hosea stood and said in a deep voice, "I will make arrangements so that you will never be at the mercy of unscrupulous persons again. If you are ever hungry, you can glean from my father's fields or help my mother in the bakery for food or money. I will never again close my doors to your basic needs." He paused, for she had turned her head away.

His voice held a note of desperation. "I did not know what else to do, Gomer, but send you away. I do not know now what else I could have done."

She did not answer, and Hosea stood looking at her helplessly. Neither had wanted to hurt the other, yet they had. Now he wondered if it could ever be mended. "Do you feel strong enough to see the children tomorrow?" he asked, wondering if she were emotionally able.

Her head came around and her eyes held his for the first time. In them was a flicker of excitement, disbelief and fear. "May I—really see them?"

"They will be here tomorrow," he said quickly, then turned from her eyes and went into the house without another word.

Chapter Twenty-Four

Gomer's sleep was fitful, for she was much too excited and fearful about the prospect of holding her children again to be able to sleep. And she was confused about Hosea's actions. She did not know what to expect. *But I am here,* she kept reminding herself, *and in my own bed.*

She fell into a deep sleep toward morning and did not awaken until the sun was high. Hosea had left the house the night before and had not returned. She took a leisurely bath and washed her hair, drying it in the sun on the roof. She let the sun fall gently on her body, making it warm and giving a healthy glow to her skin.

Her clothes, which had always been perfectly fitted, were loose and hung on her. She was too thin. She decided to wear a linen dress with simple lines that were made to conceal, rather than reveal, the body's curves. The sleeves came to her elbows, hiding the bruises that had faded to a sickening yellow. Her hair was caught back into a simple twist. She felt she looked more like a demure Hebrew woman. Perhaps that would please Hosea. She would prove she was different.

The sun brought a faint glow to her face. Excitement and anticipation stimulated the color in her cheeks. She applied a rosy tint to her lips, feeling that the unbleached white of the dress did nothing to make her appear attractive, but it made her hair seem blacker and her eyes more vividly violet.

The day seemed endless. During mid-afternoon she walked in the garden, then sat in the shade on the terrace, resting her head on the back of the lounge chair. A servant brought a cool drink.

After a while she began to feel apprehensive. Perhaps he had changed his mind. But he was a good man, she reminded herself. He would not promise one thing and do the opposite. But he was also a man who had been pushed to the limit, and she had done it. Now he was in a position to get revenge. Maybe that's what he was doing. No man could be trusted.

She fought reverting to the awful state of mind she had been in during the past terrible months. But the questions kept coming. He put her out. Why had he brought her back? Why else but to humiliate and torture her? This would be a worse torture than letting her remain at the slave market—letting her be near and never near enough.

Just as these thoughts were about to consume her, she heard voices.

She did not rise from the chair but slowly swung her feet around, placing them on the terrace. She was afraid her knees would be too weak to allow her to stand. Hosea was coming toward her holding a little boy in his arms. At first she thought it was Jezreel. But Jezreel would be older. This would have to be Loammi. He would be two years old now, almost as old as Jezreel when she saw him last. This was the one she remembered as two months old, just a newborn baby.

Hosea walked over to her. "Say hello to Mommy."

The little boy leaned forward and said, "Mommy," in a jerky manner, then laughed with pleasure at having done what he was told. He shyly put his arms around his father's neck and peered at her with sidelong glances.

Gomer wanted to grasp her child, feel him in her arms, hold his little body close to her heart, but knew she must not frighten him. Slowly she stood and reached out her hand to touch his arm. A warm, soft, chubby little arm.

"Loammi," she whispered softly and moved her fingers away, lest he feel the trembling. He looked at her curiously.

What to do? What to say? She was uncertain, and frightened that she might grasp him and never let him go. She looked at Hosea questioningly and suddenly realized how close they stood. Only a baby apart. She could almost touch him. Such a handsome, sun-bronzed man. A strong man in many ways, a man of vitality and passion for living. How could she ever thank him and God for this?

Hosea bent over and put Loammi down. The little boy toddled over to a chair and, after several failures, managed to climb up and sit on it, staring from his mother to his father and back again, contemplative.

"Loruhamah and Jezreel will be along soon," Hosea said. "They had to be washed and changed after the dust fight."

"The dust fight?" she asked, sitting back down on the lounge chair. She wouldn't have cared if they were dirty.

"Jezreel ignores his sister as much as possible," Hosea explained. "But after she kicked dust on him three times he'd had enough. So he kicked dust on her. By the time I could get to them they were both groveling in the dirt."

Gomer turned back to Loammi, who looked at her and said, "Mommy." Then he laughed delightedly and stared at her again as if trying to figure out what a mommy was.

Gomer caught her breath when the servant came through the doorway with Jezreel and Loruhamah each holding onto a hand. She let them go and Loruhamah ran over to Hosea and hugged his leg. He picked her up and held her high in the air as he had done when she was just a baby. "You're beautiful with all that dirt scrubbed away," he said. She laughed. Jezreel was walking toward them like a little man, very slowly.

"This is Mommy," Hosea said to Loruhamah. She looked at Gomer and back at Hosea, took both her hands and patted his face vigorously. "Mommy," she said.

He set her down. "Go over and say hello to Mommy."

She came over, mischief in her eyes, patted Gomer's legs and said, "Mommy." Then her little blue eyes looked straight into Gomer's. Gomer was sure she didn't know what a mommy was, either, but touched the little girl's face and hair. The spell was broken when Jezreel turned and ran back into the house.

Gomer gasped and put her hand to her mouth.

"Don't worry," Hosea said quickly, seeing the devastation on her face. "He'll be back."

"Why did he go? Doesn't he like me?"

"Not like you?" Hosea almost shouted. "He has not forgotten you. You will see."

Hosea sat down in a chair. Loruhamah went over to him, climbed into his lap, thumb in her mouth. She was tired.

Shortly Jezreel returned. He was carrying Gomer's little golden lyre that had been in her bedroom. He came up to her and stared into her face for a long time. Yes, it was there in his eyes. She knew it was impossible for him to really remember her, but something deep inside knew, she was sure. A smile touched her lips and tears brimmed her eyes.

He handed her the lyre. "Mommy sing," he said excitedly and his eyes widened. Her surprise was so great she could say nothing. Reaching out, she touched his little shoulder and he stood looking at her with wonder.

Hosea removed a protesting little girl from his lap and set her on the terrace. She lay on her back and began to kick and cry. "Now you stop that or I'll spank you," he said firmly. She puckered her little lips and glared at him, but stopped.

Hosea came over and sat by Gomer on the lounge. He took the harp from her lap. "Mommy doesn't feel like singing right now. You sing for her. All right?" He struck a cord on the lyre.

Jezreel looked suddenly shy. "Please do," Gomer encouraged. His face brightened and he began to sing the song she had sung at Hosea's parents' home years ago, the song she had sung to Jezreel many times when he was too young to make all the motions with his hands. She had laughed at his baby attempts.

"It's beautiful," she said when he had finished. Her voice was so choked she could hardly speak.

"Kiss Mommy," Hosea encouraged and Jezreel came close, put his hands on her shoulders and kissed both cheeks. She drew him to her and hugged him.

Hosea stood. "Now it's dinnertime, then to bed." He picked Loammi up, placed him on one hip, then reached down for the grouchy little girl, who was obviously still the light of her father's life.

Jezreel took the lyre, smiled at Gomer, then followed his father into the house.

When Hosea returned to the terrace, Gomer was still sitting in the same place, still staring toward the doorway where her family had gone.

"He could not have remembered that song," she said in awe.

"No," Hosea replied, standing before her. "You know how that child loved you. You remember how he cried for you the night you went away. That night I tried to comfort him, but he would not come to me. He took sides and he chose you. He was only two-and-a-half years old, but old enough to feel things, though he couldn't understand.

"The next morning was no better. He kept calling for you. I knew that to destroy Jezreel's love for you would be to destroy something wonderful and precious in him, and would place an impenetrable barrier between myself and my son. I've kept you alive to him. I've taught the others about you. They know you. Seeing you is just a formality."

He looked out into the distance and seemed to be talking to himself. "I taught them about you when I taught them their studies. I taught Jezreel the song you had sung to him so many times. We would go to your room and I would tell them how you looked, your beautiful face, your violet eyes, your black hair. I would show them your clothes, and tell them how you laughed and sang and danced. They were delighted as if I had told them a most marvelous story they never tired of hearing." He paused, now looking at her. "They know you belong here."

Gomer was so overwhelmed she could not speak. As the soft fragrances from the garden drifted over them, she wanted to fall at his feet, but sensed he would not like that.

"I don't know how all this is possible," she murmured at last. "It is far more than I ever could have hoped for. I thought everything meaningful and good was gone from me forever. Being your slave is greater than being free anywhere, with anyone, at any time."

"You are nobody's slave," he replied gruffly. "That bill of sale was destroyed the day it was made out."

She did not understand how he could be so gentle one minute and so angry the next. "Then—what do you expect of me? I did not return of my own accord. You brought me here because you felt sorry for me."

"I brought you here because you are my wife," he said forcefully, looking out over the garden. Then he added, "There is only one request I make of you. If you agree to it, this is your home for as long as you want it to be."

"That I forsake the gods I called my own?"

"Yes."

"I have done that."

"Then this is your home."

"As . . . before?"

Hosea drew in a deep breath. "I cannot guarantee that. What I want is for you to worship God Jehovah only, be a faithful wife, a loving mother, mistress of this house, and in that order. But you must do that in your own way, not mine."

"I will do my best," she assured him. "I will try."

"You have done it before and without any great effort."

"I will try to be the wife you can be proud of," she said. "Do my clothes please you? And my hair?"

"You are trying to be sensible and modest. Is that right?"

"More like the Hebrew women," she answered.

"Do not try to be a Hebrew woman," he said, using the words she had said to him many times. "I married a woman whose beauty has caused her much grief, but has given me much pleasure. Your beauty is a wonderful thing to behold and I would not want you to try to hide it. It would be a losing battle anyway." A smile hovered around his lips for an instant, then vanished.

He turned toward the house. "The children are tired and will be put to bed soon. Let's kiss them goodnight together, and then I would like for you to dine with me, if you will."

"Of course," she said as they went into the house. When the children accepted her kiss as naturally as they did their father's, she had an overwhelming sense of unreality.

"Sometimes," she whispered after they were in the hallway, "I'm afraid I will wake up and find this is a dream."

"I know the feeling," Hosea replied and walked on down the hallway.

Gomer went to her room and put on one of her finest silk gowns, and dropped her hair down below her shoulders. She wore sandals with gold straps, and gold bracelets and rings.

She pulled one side of her hair back from her face with a golden comb. She was surprised at the young woman who looked back at her from the silver mirror. She had not thought she could ever again look like that.

Later, when Hosea stared at her a long moment, she felt an unexpected shyness. During dinner she asked about Huldah and Beeri. He filled her in on their activities of the two years she had been away.

Everything was so unbelievably reminiscent of earlier, happier times, she was left not knowing what to think when, after dinner, Hosea thanked her for the evening and bid her goodnight, saying he would see her in the morning.

She could not speak even to say goodnight. She did not understand. He had acknowledged her as his wife. His eyes and his words said he wanted her here, wanted her as a part of his life. Yet he withdrew. Now she realized this was not the first time he had moved away from her when she was close. He had done that several times on the terrace. He did not want to touch her, or want her to touch him. Perhaps he had turned to another woman during her absence. The thought was so devastating she shuddered to think how she had hurt him this way in the past, without meaning to.

That was the problem, she was sure. It had been almost impossible for Hosea to accept Jothan in her life when she thought him a god. And Hosea knew she had lived with Jothan when she no longer thought him a god.

Whatever the reason, Hosea could not bear to touch her. He had not said so in words, but it could not be plainer. And she could do nothing, for she could not change the past.

Chapter Twenty-Five

Gradually Gomer involved herself with the life of the household and the children. After Loammi had been put to bed one evening, she joined Hosea for the religious instruction of Jezreel and Loruhamah. She was amazed at how much Jezreel had learned in his few short years. Then Hosea asked Loru, "Who made the stars?"

"God," she replied, but Jezreel looked at her and said, "Baal." He said it in his baby talk of years before and did not pronounce the "l," but it was unmistakable.

Gomer gasped and her hand flew to her mouth. She shook her head, looking at Hosea in desperation, but he did not appear perturbed.

"That's enough for tonight. Run along and find the nurse, Jezreel. It's bedtime."

After the children were taken from the roof, Gomer whispered, "I didn't. You must believe me. I would not tell him that."

Hosea lifted his hand. "I know that. He doesn't know what he is saying. He only knows his beloved mother taught it, and all the time you were gone it was his way of identifying with you."

"I will teach him differently," she assured him.

Hosea nodded. "Only you can do that," he said, getting up from the chair and walking over to the wall, his back to her.

"I've caused you so much unhappiness," she said, going over to him. "You should have married someone who would be better to you. Like—Marabah."

Without looking at her, he asked, "Why?"

"She would do the right things. Say the right things. Teach the children things about God that I haven't yet learned. She would be good to you."

"That sounds like my mother," he said distantly.

"Yes," Gomer replied. "She is probably good, like your mother."

After a moment's contemplation he said, "I don't think anyone could ask for a finer mother than I have. Why would I want another one?"

"Then why do you not want me anymore? Why do you give me everything I had before—except yourself?"

Hosea was thoughtful. "Many reasons," he said finally. "We have hurt each other during the past years, regardless of our intentions. It takes time to heal. I would not want to resume our close relationship unless I knew that I had all of you, all your love and respect. I will never again share you with another man. Nor would I come to you unless I knew I could give my all. I have to rid myself of the madness that threatens when I think of another man having that closeness to you."

She felt the anger in his voice. Or was it anguish? Then his voice was lower. "One of the most difficult things I've ever done is learn to live without you. But I don't think I could ever go through that again. I won't do it."

"I would not leave you again," she said softly. "I would not knowingly do anything to cause you to put me out."

Hosea turned and looked at her for a long time. "No, you

are grateful to me for bringing you home, to your beloved children." His face became very serious. "But we do not really know what we will do until we are tempted."

"But it was my belief in the gods that tempted me," she explained. "I did not mean it against you."

"Yes," he replied. "I understand that you were deceived. I can see it from your point of view. But I have to deal with it from my point of view. I was never deceived. I never for a moment thought you were a goddess. I always knew you were a woman." Then he added, "And he was a man."

Lowering her head, she turned her back to him. Jothan again. He could not forget.

"Why do you turn away?"

"Because," she said, a sob in her voice, "knowing how you think and feel makes me—ashamed."

"Turn around and look at me," he commanded.

When she turned her tear-filled eyes to him, Hosea said gently, "Don't hide that from me. I need to know that you are ashamed, that you know what kind of life that is."

"Do you want to tell me to my face that I am those dirty words you told all of Israel?"

He looked at her in surprise. "I never said anything about you to Israel. I spoke to Israel about Israel."

"How did you know I was at the slave market?"

"Jason heard it in Jerusalem and came to tell me."

"Why did you come for me?"

"Why?" Again he chose his words carefully. "When Jason came to me with his news, I hardly stopped. I just felt I had to do it. I could not let you be in a place like that."

She was afraid of the next question she had to ask. "And what was your message to Israel after you brought me here?"

"That Israel would be taken into slavery. That she would leave her beloved homeland and lose her kings and priests.

That she would become ashamed of the idols she worshiped. God has passed judgment on Israel. She will be punished for her wickedness. Israel was warned over and over but would not listen, so God will have no compassion."

Hosea again turned from her, looking out over the land. Great sorrow was in his voice. "Because Israel has rebelled against God, the land will lie desolate. Israel will fall by the sword."

Gomer asked quietly, "And that is the end of Israel?"

"That is all I know," he replied. "God has revealed nothing more to me."

Gomer was silent for awhile. "You are also waiting until God tells you what to do with me."

Hosea shook his head. "God has given me a mind. He does not dictate to me every move to make. But I cannot separate my personal life and my spiritual life. He works in and through both. I can only try to listen and obey, not evaluate and understand. I cannot explain Him and His dealings with me or with Israel. I can only try to be a fit vessel for Him to use."

Gomer felt that at the moment he had quite forgotten her. In a small voice she asked, "How will you ever know what to do with me?"

"I will know," was all he said.

Gomer turned toward the night and looked out for a long time. Finally he asked, "What are you thinking?"

"I'm not thinking," she quipped. "I'm praying." Then she turned her eyes toward him and mischief was in them.

Hosea suddenly laughed and realized what a long time it had been since he had done that.

And because they laughed together, Gomer thought perhaps it was not such a serious matter. As if reading her thoughts, Hosea turned to her and said very seriously, "You told me you would do anything I asked of you. Well, now I'm asking you—do not work against me. Help me to resist you."

"You don't trust me," she said in a choked voice. "You can't forgive me." Her words came faster and more breathless as she began to cry. "You don't love me anymore." And she covered her face with her hands.

"This is not against you," Hosea replied calmly. "It is for you. For us. For our marriage. But I see you do not understand."

She was nodding and wiping her eyes, hating the tears that never seemed to end. She had taken too much for granted. "I seem to be slow to understand," she replied. "But I do. You do not want to hold me, or kiss me, or touch me."

Hosea stared at her gravely.

"Why do you look at me like that?" she pleaded.

"I asked you to help me in this," he said as if speaking to a child. "You could start now." He walked away and left the roof.

It was not fair of him, she told herself. To treat her like an irresponsible child.

The days stretched into weeks, and the weeks into months. Gomer realized she had been waiting, questioning Hosea with her eyes, wondering if she had proved her love and faithfulness, looking for a sign that she should go to him, or that he would come to her. When they were close she would look up at him and wonder when he would ever take her into his arms again. He would notice her expression and walk away. Sometimes he would leave the house, and she feared he took another woman.

But when he returned he was not at peace, and he avoided her searching glances. She was almost positive there were times when he wanted her very much, and then he would shut himself up in his study.

On a cool afternoon before the November rains began, they were on the terrace. Loru had refused to pick up her toys and put them away for the day. Hosea picked them up. "These will not be returned to you until you can behave and obey your mommy and daddy," he told her sternly. Loru cried and pretended she thought her father didn't love her, but for the next several days her behavior was exemplary. The discipline was what she needed.

"It hurts me to do that," Hosea had said, and Gomer began to understand that his discipline of her was much the same. He found no pleasure in it. For himself, it was self-imposed punishment and she was sorry he felt it necessary to discipline her.

She had not done as he had asked. She had been hurt and resentful, taking his decision as a personal rejection. She resolved not to do that anymore. Then she remembered how she had promised God she would serve Him.

"Will you teach me all you know about God?" she asked Hosea one evening during dinner, and his reaction thrilled her. During the cold, winter months, after the children had gone to bed early, she and Hosea would sit before the lighted fire in the sitting room and study about God Jehovah. Some evenings she got so excited about the stories she would have to stop the lessons and begin writing a musical production of the story.

Gomer taught Jezreel his lessons in the mornings. She began her dance practice again, and on the cold, rainy days when Hosea stayed home he would dance with her. There were wonderful times when they sang together. She wrote children's simple productions that Jezreel and Loruhamah loved acting out and singing in. Even Loammi could take part in some of them.

The days became filled with dancing, singing, playing musical instruments, studying, writing poetry and composing music. Gomer found herself reveling in all the many blessings that belonged to her and her family.

Spring came and flowers dotted the hillsides. They walked with the children and taught them the names of flowers, trees and shrubs, and who made them. Sometimes Hosea and Gomer walked alone in the hills and occasionally went to their old meeting place above the well.

Late one afternoon they were there, looking about at the beauty of life bursting into bloom. As they waited for the sunset, Hosea stared at the beautiful, talented Gomer, now a loving mother and contented wife, and his heart throbbed with pride and love.

She seems almost like the little girl I met here many years ago, he thought. *And yet she is more. She is my wife.*

Hosea put his arm around her waist and felt her tremble. They stood silently for a long time. Then she said, "Isn't it strange that we do not know the value of something until we have lost it? Don't you suppose that is why God says Israel must lose this glorious land? Only then will the people know who gave it to them in the first place, and they will know how they should have valued it and cared for it and not taken it for granted."

Her words came faster. "Today I can thank God for everything He ever gave me, and took from me. And Hosea, I can even thank you for all you gave me. And took from me."

"My darling," he said suddenly, and drew her close. He had not held her like this in a long time and did not ever want to let her go. After a while they walked back home in the dwindling light.

"I must put my thoughts into poetry," she said excitedly. "If I do it well, perhaps others will be saved from much anguish and will learn more of God." She smiled at him. "That's why you do it, isn't it?"

"Yes," he replied. "We must try to share what we learn and know about God."

"You are happy," she said.

"I am," he replied. "I cannot imagine anyone more blessed than I."

"I believe there are a couple of gray hairs at your temples, Hosea," she joked, clicking her tongue and touching his hair.

"Well, what can you expect of an old man of thirty?"

She withdrew her hand, laughing with him. "It gives you quite a look of distinction. But you've always been so . . . good-looking."

Watching her as she ascended the stairs to check on the children, Hosea wondered why he still held himself in reserve from her. There seemed to be no reason anymore. And yet something inside told him to hold back. He did not know why, but had learned that he must not act without a certainty in his mind. And he did not have that.

Chapter Twenty-Six

As soon as Hosea returned from Jerusalem he bathed, changed his clothes and joined Gomer on the terrace. The sun had set, the stars were brilliant and the moon almost full. The terrace lamps were lighted and a cool evening breeze was gently blowing.

Hosea talked about his trip, about events in Jerusalem, about the message he had delivered to the people. "We will soon be a nation of slaves in a foreign land," he said. "Although the people are being warned, they cannot believe it."

Gomer always struggled to understand her husband's prophetic gifts. She shivered at his gloomy prediction. "How soon will it happen?" she asked.

"It is already beginning to happen," he explained. "Assyria and Egypt are draining our nation. But they are not the ones. We can look for the rise of Babylon. Individuals may repent, but God's judgment has already been passed on the nation. His wrath is upon us."

She accepted his words as truth. Some of the things he had prophesied in the past had already happened. She searched for some meaning for her own life in his words, but only one thought came through—he was so disgusted with her past actions that he could never call her his bride again, at least not in a physical way. One did not change God's mind, and one did not change Hosea's mind. She felt a chill go through her.

"Another thing I learned," he said. "Beniah has been banished from the temple. He is no longer a High Priest. He has been formally charged with misuse of funds and of young temple assistants."

"That is not surprising," she said, and felt herself tremble at memories she had tried to push from her mind.

"The temple at Tyre has grown so large that Jothan and Rizpah have been sent back to Bethel to rebuild what Beniah has damaged," Hosea continued. "They will remain there until a new High Priest can be appointed and appropriate action taken against Beniah."

Gomer did not look up from her hands that were clasped on her lap. She was grateful for the near darkness and hoped it would hide the color she knew came to her face. She wished she did not have to be reminded so much of the past. Knowing Hosea was watching her made her uncomfortable. He would try to read her expression. He always did that. Breathing deeply, she looked helplessly toward the heavens and her eyes lingered on the almost full moon. Tomorrow night it would be full. There would be a new moon festival at the temple.

Suddenly she knew what she must do. A light came into her eyes as she looked toward Hosea. "May I go and see them?"

He looked at her sharply, obviously aware of the excitement in her voice. "You do as you please," he said with effort, forcing his voice to sound harsh. "But you must remember. My conditions for your being here as my wife will never change."

Gomer went over and knelt in front of him, her arms on his knees, and looked up at him. She felt him stiffen at her touch and a hard expression came onto his face. "Don't be angry with me, Hosea. I don't want to do as I please. I want to please you. All you have to do is say no and everything will be as before."

"No," he replied. "It will not be as before. I would never forget that you asked."

Her face was sad. "Rizpah is the only family I have left. The last time I saw her, we were not on good terms." She felt his muscles tighten beneath her hands. "Will you go with me?" She wished now that she had not asked. "Just yes or no," she pleaded.

"Go," he said. He raised her to her feet, put his arms around her and drew her near, so roughly she gasped, then lay her head against his chest. Just as suddenly he dropped his arms, turned and walked hastily toward the house.

Gomer wanted to explain further, but did not see him for the remainder of the evening. What explanation could she give, anyway?

The following morning Gomer was putting baked goods into a basket to take to Rizpah and her children. Her own children were helping her. The night before she and the servants had baked the delicacies that Huldah had taught her.

Hosea had not left for work. Normally he would have gone by now. Gomer handed him a pastry. "We made these last night," she said.

He sampled it, lifted his eyebrows. "Almost as good as Mother's," he commented.

"Almost?" she laughed. "It's the same recipe."

Gomer knew his eyes were probing but she could not look directly at him. Many things were in her mind. She had lain awake a long time remembering his arms about her in a most possessive way. There had been a sense of desperation in his grasp, and her heart went out to him, wishing she could put away his doubts. Perhaps she never could.

"Of course you won't let the children go," Gomer said.

"Need you ask?" he replied and she realized that was why he had not gone to work, to ensure she did not take the children.

"I did not ask," she replied, and paused in front of him at the doorway. "I am taking two servants with me," she said. "You can ask them what we did after we return."

"I would not do that."

"I know," she said. "But you could." Then she looked up at him pleadingly. "Trust me." Standing in front of him she again remembered his arms about her and almost wished he would do that now and refuse to let her go. But he made no move toward her.

He and the children watched as she and the two servants walked across the court and out the gate toward the waiting cart. Turning at the gate, she waved and they waved back.

As Hosea turned to the empty house, his spirits were low. Even the children were strangely subdued. Could he face the future without her? How could he live without her laughter, her singing, her dancing, her charm, her beauty, her quick mind that never accepted anything without question? He did not think it would be any easier this time.

Yet he was reasonably sure she did not want to be a part of her past life anymore, that she knew the gods of Baal were idols. She knew Jothan was a man, not a god. Perhaps she was going to him because he was a man. She was a warm, loving person and needed a man. Perhaps he should not have deprived her of lovemaking.

And he had not told her he would put her out of the house if she went to other men. He had said she could not go to idols. Suppose she went to Jothan, then returned to her home and her children? What would he do? She had once told him he was wise and strong. Suddenly he felt anything but wise and strong.

Later in the afternoon, when he went to her room, he saw that the statue of Ashtoreth was gone. Why had she taken her former goddess with her? She had asked for him to trust her. He was not doing very well.

He left the children in the servants' care, walked through the hills to the place where he and Gomer had fallen in love and had such wonderful, sweet times. Returning to the house, he remembered their first year of marriage, so full of love for each other, a passionate year when there seemed to be no one in the world except the two of them. And they had made a child together. Then her relatives had come. That had been the beginning of the end.

These past several months during the harvest, the rains, the winter and the spring had been so good. But she was walking directly into temptation. How strong was she now?

The sun was fast departing and he knew that soon the moon would be high and full. He would have to go somewhere so he would not see it.

Chapter Twenty-Seven

The cart stopped outside the palace gates. Gomer got out and made her way around to the back courtyard. The sounds of children playing and laughing, their voices as light as the cool spring morning, brought memories of her own carefree, happy childhood. Undetected, she stood for a moment in the shadow of a fragrant flowering arbor.

Rizpah stood in front of Jothan to brush away a speck of lint from his black robe, then lifted her face for a brief parting kiss. The children in turn came to their father for a hug and kiss as he knelt before them.

Rizpah's surprised exclamation of "Gomer!" temporarily suspended all activity. The children looked in the direction of their mother's gaze. Jothan was the first to move. He rose from his kneeling position and stood staring at her. Rizpah's eyes seemed to ask why Gomer was there.

Gomer stepped forward. "I came for a visit, Rizpah."

Rizpah went to her and they embraced. "Come and meet your nieces and nephews," Rizpah said, smiling, but Gomer detected the same constraint in her voice that had been in her embrace. "Jothan was just leaving for the temple."

"I'll be there all day, Gomer," he said casually. "Stop by and see me before you leave."

Gomer did not acknowledge his glance as he walked past

her, but as she smiled toward the children, who had resumed their activity, she knew in an instant that her major reason for being here was not to see Rizpah or her children.

Later in the morning, after dispensing with trivialities, Rizpah said seriously, "So he took you back. How could he?"

"He loves me," Gomer replied softly.

Rizpah smiled faintly and a distant light shone in her eyes. "There's something special about him. I'm not sure what it is."

"I can't explain him fully," Gomer said in response to the question in Rizpah's eyes. "But I do know there's an assurance in his life that most of us search for and never find. God's Spirit dwells in him, speaks to him. He doesn't just hope God is with him. He knows it. It motivates all his life and actions.

"And Rizpah," Gomer added intently, "he knows the one true God."

Rizpah stared at Gomer for a long time, then said slowly, "I knew it was something, but I didn't know what."

"He's loving and forgiving," Gomer said softly, "because God is that way."

Rizpah inhaled deeply, then smiled. "Well, whatever. It certainly agrees with you. You look marvelous. Now tell me about your children."

After much discussion, Gomer commented, "You seem happier than I've ever known you to be, Rizpah."

"I am," Rizpah said, smiling. "Since I retired from the temple I devote my time to home and family, and love every minute of it. I never thought I would. Jothan likes my being home, too. Oh, there's entertaining and occasional travel, so it's not a matter of my being absorbed by children only. I'm more content than I've ever been, Gomer."

When the sisters parted, Gomer felt Rizpah's embrace was genuine. She knew Rizpah could not yet trust her, but this was a beginning. They would talk again.

Gomer took the golden statue wrapped in a soft cloth from the picnic basket, and walked toward the temple of Baal. Entering through the front doorway, she looked around. So many memories here!—her years of training and dancing, the ceremonies, Hosea's violent actions, and even Beniah. She shivered.

The last time she was here, she had seen the temple through eyes of confusion, hurt and anger at her gods. Violet eyes traveled around the golden, gleaming structure before a movement caught her eyes. With elegant grace, she walked across the white marble floor and up the gold-carpeted steps to where Jothan stood outside his private chambers waiting for her.

When she entered his chambers and the curtains closed behind them, she realized memory knew no time. It was all there, the times spent here with Jothan.

He led her to the couches in the corner. "It's good to see you well and happy again, Gomer," Jothan said, pouring wine into two goblets and bringing them over to the table. He sat across from her.

Wasting no words, he began, "Come back, Gomer. I will choose my mate tonight for the festival. But I'm offering you more than that. You would be High Priestess not only here, but in Tyre." His eyes showed his excitement at the thought. "You would be queen of all the goddesses. More famous than any of the others."

"And what of Rizpah, Jothan?" she asked quietly.

"The temple practices are more important than Rizpah," he said dutifully. How well she knew the tone! "Our home is entirely separate now. We both prefer it that way."

Once he had been her god. The images had been her gods. She had felt a strange sensation when she had spoken to

Rizpah about God Jehovah, and now she delighted in the words that came from her lips.

"The Lord God says that you shall not make any graven image, or bow down to idols," she said easily. "Yours are manmade, Jothan, and an abomination to God."

"Well," he said, turning the wine goblet in his fingers, a wry smile on his lips. "It seems that prophet has poisoned your mind."

"I suppose," Gomer smiled. "It's sort of like the powder we put on our plants in the garden. The powder represents protection and security against being ravaged by insects, and makes the garden grow beautiful and strong and healthy." She tried to make her voice sound light. "Only to the vermin is it poison."

"Some of that powder must have been sprinkled on you." His black eyes bore into hers and the smile left her face. "You seem stronger and healthier and more beautiful than ever before."

Looking away from his steady gaze, she carefully unwrapped the lovely golden statue and set it in front of him.

"What shall I do with it?" he asked.

"I don't know," she said quietly. "But I want you to have it. It's my way of saying that this is a part of my life that is over. This," she said, gazing at the statue, "can be our symbol of closing the door to the past."

"Impossible," he murmured. "In the past you've come to me as a child, as a goddess, and as a woman, with never a door closed. If you find you wish to come to me tonight, tomorrow, next week, next year, or ever—you will still find no closed doors to prevent it." He stood to refill his glass.

Gomer stood, too, and without a parting word left the room. There was one other thing she must do before leaving the temple. She talked to the young girls, excited about the evening's activities. They listened intently when Gomer began to tell them she had once been like them, a part of temple activities. They listened in awe, for she was beautiful, and her voice like that of an angel.

"But I found there is only one true God," Gomer said after gaining their attention. "It is God Jehovah. I know it's hard for you to listen now, but if you ever come to a point in your life when you wonder, when you question, remember my words."

"She is right," a voice sounded behind Gomer and she stiffened. Jothan stood in the doorway and all the young beauties stared in wonder. Gomer knew how they felt. It was in their eyes and face as they stared at the magnificent man who, to them, was a god. "God Jehovah is a great god," Jothan assured them. "Worship him if you like. Our gods are not jealous. Even tonight, our temple will be filled with Jehovah-worshipers who come to celebrate with us."

His triumphal gaze met Gomer's and she knew he was feeling like a god again. She also suspected it was not her words but Jothan's that registered in the young girls' minds.

Hosea heard footsteps on the terrace and told himself it was a servant. "Rizpah sends her love," she said softly, and it was not a servant's voice. A joy engulfed him. He turned and listened to her account of the visit with Rizpah and the things she had said about God.

"Do you think she believed you?" Hosea asked.

"If she does, she will keep it to herself. She could hardly declare it openly. But it's a step forward, Hosea. And she doesn't—hate me anymore." Gomer paused and said quickly, "I'm hot and dusty and need to bathe before dinner. We can talk then."

During dinner Gomer talked about Rizpah's children, how they looked, how old they were. "Four of them now," she said. "They're beautiful, but not as beautiful as ours. Or as well-behaved." She laughed. "Or as smart."

Hosea laughed with her.

Gomer did not volunteer any more information and they finished the meal in silence. After dinner, Hosea suggested they go onto the roof.

The full moon shone so brightly it was almost day. They sat in silence. Gomer knew he would not ask, but the question would always be between them until she answered it. "I saw Jothan at the temple after leaving Rizpah."

She saw the rise of his shoulders. "And how is he?"

"The same. Very charming. His harem of young girls—ages thirteen, fourteen, fifteen—find him fascinating. They adore him. He is their god." Then Gomer told him the things she had said to him about God, and what she had told the young girls. "I loved talking about God," she said. Indeed, he noticed a difference about her, a glow, a certain look in her eyes. "It was like a confirmation of God's reality." She paused a moment. "And I returned the statue of Ashtoreth to Jothan."

"Why?" he asked.

"It was a symbol of a way of life that is over," she assured him. "I have no further use for that object. It is no longer my god."

There was a lengthy silence. "Why do you look at me like that?" she finally asked, uncomfortable.

"Just waiting for you to finish," he said quietly.

"I—I did finish," she said.

He shook his head. "A man spends several years with you, intimates you are more important than his wife, offers you the best of his world, and you hand it back to him. Surely he at least must have thanked you."

Lest he think she was trying to hide something, she told him what Jothan had said.

"And his open invitation disturbs you?" Hosea asked.

"Yes," she admitted. "I felt so wonderful when I acknowledged God. And I thought I could say this is over, and it would be. It would have been much simpler if Jothan had agreed and closed the door."

"Are you afraid you'll go back?"

"No," she said quickly, a light in her eyes. "Not afraid. But what disturbed me was a realization. A few years ago the idea that I would ever turn from my gods was ridiculous. But I did that. I realized today that I cannot honestly say, *I will, I won't, I can, I can't.* It isn't so simple. There are many open doorways that lead away from God, or toward Him. I know what desperation can do to a person. I don't hate Jothan. If you were to put me out again, I might go to him."

She watched Hosea's reaction and he did not seem angry. Looking up at the full moon she said, "They are into their festival now."

Hosea's eyes caressed her face. "You're new to the faith, Gomer, but you spoke out for God three times today. You were faced with temptations that you resisted. Then you hurried back to me."

She could not take her eyes from his. "That tells you . . . something . . . doesn't it?" she asked in a whisper.

"Something?" he said, moving to the edge of the couch and reaching for her hands. "My darling! It tells me a great deal!"

"Then you must know how much I love you," she said, unable to keep the longing for him out of her voice.

Hosea placed his hand against her cheek. "I need and want your love very much. Please be patient with me."

During the following days Hosea spent much of his time in deep contemplation. Then one evening when they had almost finished with dinner he said suddenly, "I would like for you to go to Jerusalem with me."

Gomer looked at him quickly. To go away for awhile, just the two of them. She dared not let him see the excitement she knew would show on her face, so she looked down at the food on her plate.

"Why Jerusalem?" she said finally.

"It would be a nice trip for us," he said, watching her closely. "Also, I thought Jason and Marabah might go with us."

She hoped the sudden disappointment did not show. But he noticed. "What's wrong?"

Gomer knew she must tell the truth. "I just don't know if we would enjoy it with them along."

"Jason is my closest friend."

"I know. But Marabah is not mine. She doesn't like me and I cannot help but remember that she was my rival for you."

"You talk foolishness," he said gruffly. "Don't you know that from the moment I first saw you, you had no rival? No competition? There never has been and never can be a woman to compare with you."

Gomer caught her breath. He had a way of making his compliments sound like reprimands. "However," he said, "since you must constantly be reassured. . . ." His voice trailed off and he stood. "I'll be right back." He left the room.

Shortly he returned. He handed her a small golden box, on top of which was the figure of a tiny golden dove. With a delighted exclamation she opened the box. On violet-colored velvet were two mother-of-pearl combs and a golden ring with a mother-of-pearl stone.

Tears sprang to her eyes as she looked at him in wonder. "So beautiful," she murmured, closing the top and touching the dove.

Then Hosea took her hand and placed the ring on her finger where her wedding ring had been, before she had sold it.

Not knowing what to say, she whispered in awe, "Where did you get these gifts?"

After a moment's hesitation, Hosea answered, "Almost three years ago. In Jerusalem."

Almost three years ago! That would have been the time he had gone to Jerusalem and she had gone to the temple after he warned her he would put her out. "How can you not despise me?" she asked.

Hosea moved behind her and his hand rested on the soft skin of her neck. She could feel his hand tremble against the throbbing vein in her throat. He bent low and she felt his breath against her ear. "My beautiful dove. Don't you know?" he said, his voice a hoarse whisper. "I love you."

Just as quickly he straightened, rested his hand briefly on her shoulder, then turned and left the room.

Gomer did not know how long she sat there. It must have been a long time, for a servant came and asked if she would like her to light another candle. She told her no and realized her face was wet with unchecked tears. She found him in his bedroom and stood at the doorway until he felt her presence.

"Thank you," she said.

Hosea smiled and saw in her face the joy, the adoration of the little girl at the well so long ago.

Chapter Twenty-Eight

Marabah felt ashamed of herself. Jason had asked her many times to visit Hosea and Gomer with him. "I wouldn't know what to say to a woman like that," she had replied.

"You should not speak of her that way, Marabah," he had chided gently but firmly. "She is a woman like you, like anyone else. It is not her fault she was raised to believe in Baalism. She has left that now. God does not want us to put ourselves above other people."

"I know that with my mind, Jason," she said. "But I can't go into their home and pretend to like her just because you and Hosea are friends and you want me to be her friend. I'm sorry."

Jason had smiled his sad smile. "I'm glad you're honest with me, Marabah. I know we can't push friendships on each other."

Another time Jason had told her how much he liked a musical play Gomer had written and how, like her first one, it had been accepted by the High Priest at the Temple in Jerusalem.

"It's amazing how creative Gomer is with her music in teaching their children," Jason said admiringly.

Marabah wondered if she would ever have children. "They're very blessed," she had commented stonily.

"Yes, they are. But few people could have survived their trials. And it must be difficult not to have any friends."

"She seems happy enough when she comes to Huldah's. I've seen her in the bakery many times," Marabah retorted shortly.

"Yes," Jason replied. "I'm sure she can survive without them, because she has Hosea, her children, her in-laws, and a new faith in God. Those who get to know God as an adult are often more excited about Him and more devout than some of us who have known Him all our lives. Did you know, Marabah, that Huldah prayed fervently for Gomer to turn to God since the first time she met her? Now Huldah is comparing Gomer to Ruth who was a Moabite and did not know God Jehovah until she was an adult. Yet God allowed her to be the grandmother of King David."

It was true, Marabah had to admit, that Hosea's and Gomer's children seemed to know more about God than other children their age. And their musical accomplishments were amazing. None of her friend's children played musical instruments at such an early age. Secretly she admitted she would like her children to be like that, if she ever had any.

Then once Jason had said a frightening thing. He was talking about Israel's being taken into slavery according to Hosea's prediction. "The reason," he said pointedly, "is not because of the pagans. It is because we as God's chosen people know what God demands, yet we refuse to obey Him."

Marabah had shuddered. God's judgment was not because of Gomer's kind of people, but her own kind—the Israelites. God's chosen people. She felt her own stab of guilt. She had never prayed for Gomer, although Huldah had asked her to.

She had begun to pray about her feelings and to think about what it meant to be a friend. Being a friend meant you did not talk against that person; you did not harbor resentment and you shared together about personal matters. At first she wondered if she really wanted Gomer as a friend. Later she began to wonder if she could be a friend to Gomer, or if Gomer would even want her friendship.

Then all those thoughts had been pushed aside by a marvelous discovery. She and Jason were going to have a child. They were ecstatic and their relationship took on a different quality. She had been forced to see herself as a rather domineering personality, but now that she was pregnant, Jason treated her as though she were fragile. She didn't mind this a bit.

"Hosea and Gomer are going to Jerusalem," he said after a visit to their house. "They would like us to go with them." His look was expectant. "Of course, if it would be too hard on you. . . ."

Marabah laughed. "I rather think it would be good for me. After all, I hardly show. And I want everyone to know."

"Then you'll go?" he asked excitedly. Something in his tone made her want to please him.

"I'll go," she said.

Hosea greeted them warmly. Then he took Marabah's hands and said, "I'm especially glad you came to visit us, Marabah." She returned the smile, feeling comfortable with him in a new way. He had always acted toward her as if she was a dear sister. She now felt as if he were a dear brother.

"Gomer is putting the children to bed," Hosea explained. Then he asked his guests to be seated in the sitting room.

When Gomer entered a few minutes later, Marabah felt herself stiffen. In the presence of Gomer's beauty she felt plain, second-best. Would she ever be able to get over her resentment toward this woman who had achieved what she could not?

Smiling at her guests, Gomer apologized. "Loammi was

fussy tonight and wanted me to sing to him before he went to sleep."

Marabah took a firm grip on herself. "I've heard Jezreel sing the stories of David and Jonathan and Abraham and Moses. The other children listen to him and he teaches them to make motions with their hands."

Gomer smiled. "He's quite a little actor, and a poet at heart. He learns and remembers the stories if they have rhythm."

"That's the way you teach your children, isn't it?" Marabah asked her, interested.

"The rhythms make our learning times enjoyable as well as instructional. Otherwise children get bored so quickly."

Hosea broke in. "Some evenings we have our children dance and sing and act out what Gomer has taught them." His glance toward Gomer was one of pride.

"Jason," Marabah said, turning her face toward him, "we will soon have to decide how best to teach our children." She lay her hand gently on her stomach.

"Oh, Marabah, you're expecting?" Gomer asked joyfully.

Marabah nodded.

"How truly wonderful," exclaimed Hosea. "At dinner we will say a blessing for the unborn baby."

Marabah basked for a moment in their congratulations, then asked hesitantly, "Gomer, have you considered teaching other children? I mean, in the way you teach your own?"

"I have considered it," she said, looking at Marabah with sadness in her eyes. "But I don't really think any Hebrew women would allow me to teach their children."

Embarrassed, Marabah felt the color come into her face. She was not used to such honesty among her friends.

"I understand how Hebrew women must feel about me," Gomer said quickly. "And I could not expect them to accept me readily. Perhaps never. They would fear I would lead their children away from God."

"You're right," Marabah said after a while, to the surprise of her audience. "We accept gossip too quickly. We're too slow to help anyone who does not believe as we do. We are too suspicious and quick to criticize."

Marabah found herself unexpectedly drawn toward this woman she had so hated and vilified only months before. "You have been honest with me, Gomer, and I will be honest with you. I have been one of those who not only criticized you but had angry feelings against you. I want you to know I no longer feel that way."

There was a moment of uncomfortable silence while everyone's eyes were on Gomer. For a moment she appeared stunned, then she quickly went over to Marabah and took Marabah's hands in her own. "I'm glad to hear you say that, Marabah. I was afraid you were so perfect we could never be friends."

"You will probably discover that I'm far from perfect."

"Not too far," Jason said, smiling. Marabah felt the blush on her cheeks.

"Have you ever worn your hair up, Marabah?" Gomer asked unexpectedly. "It's so thick and lovely. I think it would suit you."

"No," Marabah said with an amused gleam in her eyes. "Perhaps you could show me how."

"I'd love to."

"Women talk," Jason said. The two men rose from their chairs and went outside to the terrace.

When dinner was called, the two women walked slowly down the staircase. Gomer had used two golden combs on each side of Marabah's head to hold back the curls piled high on top. Little ringlets curled about her face and at the back of her neck. Marabah looked years younger.

"Who is this dazzling creature?" Jason quipped.

"Oh, Jason," she said. "Do you like it?"

"Very much," he assured her, a twinkle in his eye.

"Could I wear it this way in Jerusalem?"

"It would be perfect for Jerusalem."

It was during dinner that Hosea sprang his surprise on Gomer. "We will not be returning with you from Jerusalem," he said to Marabah.

Gomer looked at him, startled, her wine goblet held in midair. Glancing at her, Hosea continued, "Gomer and I will be taking a trip down the Nile and into Egypt."

"How long will you be gone?" Jason asked.

"Until we decide to return," Hosea remarked. "This is a pleasure trip. My parents have agreed to stay with the children as long as needed."

So he had been planning it for quite some time, Gomer thought. With the ring on her finger, the presents, his recent attention, his words of endearment, she felt like an engaged woman soon to be married.

Chapter Twenty-Nine

By the time Hosea had ascended to the altar of sacrifice outside the Temple, a large crowd had gathered in the courtyard.

"Hear the word of the Lord," Hosea's voice boomed. With pride, Gomer watched as her husband, arms held high, his long robe blowing gently in the breeze, stood before the people.

"As your God, I am your strength and protection in times of trouble. Yet you have not turned to Me, but to false gods. This has made Me sad, for when Israel was a child I loved him and brought him out of Egypt. I trained him as an infant. I taught Israel how to walk. I held him in My arms. But now he doesn't know or care that it was I who raised him.

"Israel has not planted the seeds of righteousness, but has cultivated wickedness. You people of Israel have turned from Me and taken false gods. As your Father I must punish you. Therefore the terrors of war shall rise among you. The enemy will crash through your gates. You will be enslaved and returned to Egypt and Assyria because you would not return to Me."

Hosea paused a moment as an angry rumble broke out in the crowd. Yet today Hosea's face was not ashen gray nor his eyes glazed with pain. Instead his eyes were calm, even gentle as he spoke again.

"God's message for us today is still grim, but there is more. Thus saith the Lord: I have loved you, O Israel, and I will not give up on you. I will not abandon you. For you will seek Me again and I will hear your voice."

Then Hosea's voice softened, and Gomer was certain his next words were for her only, for he smiled and looked in her direction. "Israel will again be God's bride."

As Hosea looked out over the people and toward the hills of Jerusalem, his words became charged with enthusiasm. "In time Israel will flourish like a garden and become as famous as the wine of Lebanon. The people will have deep roots and will blossom like flowers. They will grow tall and straight like the trees of Lebanon. They will flourish under My protection, saith the Lord. And I will be to the people of Israel like rain in a dry land."

As Hosea walked down the steps, the crowd began to break into small groups, discussing, arguing, gesticulating. A few voiced dissent. Who was Hosea to hear these words from God? Hadn't he refused his priestly vows? Hadn't he been involved with Baalism? What about his wife?

When some women began to criticize Hosea, Gomer suddenly spoke up. "I am Hosea's wife," she said, "so let me answer your questions."

The women eyed her cynically. "She's not one of us," one remarked. "Why should we believe her?"

"Let her speak," said another.

Gomer turned and looked gratefully at Marabah, who had come by her side. Without that sudden support, Gomer would have felt ready to run away.

"What Hosea said about false gods is true," she began

nervously. "I know, because I used to be a follower of Baal. In fact, I was High Priestess in the temple at Bethel."

At that point she had the complete attention of her audience. Others soon joined them, including Hosea. Not knowing what else to do, and with growing conviction, Gomer told the story of her involvement with Baalism, the grasp it had had on her life, the difficulties of breaking from it.

"Your God Jehovah has become as real to me as He is to Hosea. I know now He is the one true God. He does love us; I can feel His love. He has told us how to live. When we obey His laws, life is filled with joy and happiness. When we disobey Him, we reap misery and unhappiness. I have found this to be true in my life with Hosea."

Later, when they were having lunch, Marabah mentioned the morning incident. "It must have been hard for you, Gomer, but you expressed yourself beautifully," she said admiringly.

"I didn't intend to say anything," Gomer admitted. "It was as if I couldn't help it. I just hoped I would not be a further embarrassment to Hosea."

"You did not embarrass me; you made me weep with joy," Hosea replied.

In the afternoon they met with a few friends, walked the streets of Jerusalem and visited shops in the marketplace.

At one point Marabah drew Gomer aside, asking if she would mind bringing her a few choice pieces of jewelry from Egypt. "Something for my hair," she said, glancing toward the men as if not wanting Jason to hear.

Gomer laughed with her. "It is becoming, Marabah. And Jason likes it. Let me show you a few things with makeup after we get to the house tonight."

"Didn't Hosea tell you?" Marabah asked, surprised. "Jason and I won't be staying at the house with you."

"No," Gomer said. "He didn't tell me."

Marabah leaned close. "I've never felt at home in Jason's house here in Jerusalem. It reminds me of his first wife. He knows how I feel, so when we're here we stay with friends, if possible. I hope you don't mind."

"I don't mind at all," Gomer replied quickly.

Later that night, after a fragrant bath, Gomer slipped into a thin silk gown and went onto the roof, where a gentle breeze stirred the warmth of the evening. Soon Hosea joined her, his hair still damp from his bath.

Leading her to a low, long couch beside the wall, Hosea admitted, "I'm nervous. It's been so long."

"I know," she said, "but isn't it true that God will restore Israel unto Himself completely, forgiving all her past iniquities, bringing her to her former glory without restraint?"

"Of course it's true," Hosea replied confidently. "He gave that word to me."

"I thought you were talking about me," she said softly.

"I was talking about Israel," he replied, smiling. "Who are you going to believe, me or you?"

"I usually believe myself," she retorted playfully, turning toward him. "I think you are going to restore me to yourself, unconditionally, without restraint."

"What makes you so sure?" he jested.

"Everyone knows that the mark of a true prophet of God is that every word he speaks comes true."

He could say no more, for her warm hand had found its way inside his robe and lay against his heart. He found her waiting lips and yielding body.

As they came together, it was as if golden calves and graven images were being smashed in high places and in shady groves, and the sky was suddenly ablaze with a glorious sunset that streaked the sky in brilliance. Once again their love was complete, human and divine.

Later, cradled in each other's arms, blanketed by the stars that God had made, Hosea laughed lightly when Gomer said in her soft, musical voice, "You are a true prophet."